THE
COUNT

THE
COUNT

A NOVEL

ROD TAYLOR

atmosphere press

I dedicate this novel to my wife, Janice Katherine Taylor,
who had to put up with me all the time I was writing,
who was a driving force in the family, and who now, sadly,
is no longer with us.

Contents

Part 3

PART
ONE

CHAPTER 1

A Start in Life

In 1971, the stock market was growing dramatically, and property values were also soaring. Nicholas Cameron went to be interviewed for a job at the American Bank.

The bank director, Mr. Lutz, looked long and hard at his application. "So you have a degree in Mathematics? At Bristol? And then you went to Harvard? And got an MBA?"

Nick nodded. Lutz was a smallish American with a pasty face and thick glasses. He appeared to put on an air of superior confidence that Nick thought probably covered up a real lack of confidence.

"But Russian? How is it that you studied Russian as a secondary subject at University?"

Nick had been asked this many times before. "My mother is Russian, or was Russian. She is now British. She likes to talk to me in Russian. So I have kept it up and thought it could come in useful in international finance."

"It might. It might, one day. But right now we are facing a soaring stock market, and a nonstop climb in property values. Many of our clients are making fortunes, and need our advice and help in how to save their gains and how to invest."

Nick was cautious in his replies.

Lutz went on to question him about his limited experience. Then switched back to the mother. "How long has your mother lived in Britain?"

"Since the end of the war."

"What was she doing in the war? Why did she come to England?"

"I really don't know. She doesn't like talking about the past. She loves being in England. She came because she married a Scottish doctor – my father."

"I see. I see. Interesting story."

· · • • ·

Three years later, in 1974, Nick had never yet been asked to use his Russian. He was admired for his dedicated and disciplined approach to work. But not for his Russian.

And the US was now facing the fact that their President, Nixon, was expecting impeachment for his involvement in the break-in at Watergate and had resigned. Nick kept his nose down to the grindstone. This was tough since the London stock market, which had reached an all-time high of 520, had now collapsed to 140, and property values that had been growing at ten percent a month were now unsaleable.

Nick's boss, Frank Lutz, called Nick in. "Nick, we need someone with your dedication and impeccable trustworthiness to help us manage the avalanche of collapsed values and bad debts. The smart boys who put together most of these deals cannot be relied upon to sort the problems out. You have not been tainted by these serious mistakes."

Nick nodded. And wondered how Lutz had managed to avoid being corralled in with the smart boys.

Lutz had a natural lack of charm that went well with his very ordinary appearance. From a simple lower middle-class background, he did not even have the story of a shoeless childhood with ten brothers sleeping in one bed to demonstrate his remarkable ability to climb the social ladder. He had clawed his way through an ordinary college and on to the bottom rungs of the bank in a branch in upstate New York. He dug his way through the bank by being diligent, unimaginative, and reeking of sincerity. He turned up on time, had copious notes ready, always a file in good order, and could always find the right paper at the right time in a hectic meeting. He worked long hours, wrote long memos that no one read, but everyone referred to a year later when things went wrong, and he never let go of a subject.

Nick was reliable, according to the more dynamic bankers around, and was not tainted by some of the Bank's past mistakes, and that's why, when it all went wrong, he was put on to sorting out some of the bad loans. The smart boys who had put together the deals had disappeared back into the woodwork, and it was left to the innocents like Nick to try to sort things out.

Nick went back to his office that he shared with Jonathan King, a new but impressive recruit. He had a good degree from a good college at Cambridge and lots of charm. He was tall with boyish good looks and a classical English air of amused diffidence. His suits already had trousers with moderately flared legs.

Despite his immense education, Jonathan was almost totally innumerate and would never have been hired by the bank in New York. Nick did all his numbers for him in his company analyses and presentations to clients. But Jonathan was not asked to do many of those. It was who he knew and how he handled them that mattered to the bank.

Nick wondered why Jonathan, with his complete lack of any banking experience, had been recruited by Lutz. He heard that Lutz had met Jonathan at a US Embassy party, and so envied the languid Englishman's ease, style, and wit that he decided he needed him. Jonathan moved among the rich and powerful and had written several witty and analytical articles about how the wealthy did not know how to spend their wealth. Jonathan appeared on several TV chat shows where his languid, diffident style was a little lost beside sparkling film stars and abrasive pop musicians.

Lutz apparently envied Jonathan's style and valued his contacts, and couldn't resist the idea of having someone so superior as his subordinate. He must have sold the idea to the committee in New York. Jonathan clearly liked the salary size and probably had difficulty pretending he had difficulty deciding to say yes. Now Jonathan apparently helped oil the wheels that Frank would otherwise have tripped over.

"Jonathan," said Nick, "I've been asked to handle a large portion of the current bad debts that are building up."

"Good luck. Just ignore all mine that appear, will you?" he joked.

"I'm astonished to meet clients who were paper millionaires on Friday, but come back from a champagne weekend at the new country estate to find they are now bankrupt."

Jonathan smirked, "Very upsetting."

"Some of the bankrupts take it well. They hadn't had the wealth long enough to believe it and had survived on the flush of excitement of each new deal. Others had embedded themselves in the lifestyle of success and had begun to believe in themselves as self-made architects of a new financial generation, of having a sure intuitive hand in each creative new deal. Those found it hard to readjust. They couldn't believe that the bailiff was about to call."

"I bet they continue to order cases of Moet from Fortnum's well after it is too late."

"Yes, but as reality dawns, it begins to show on their faces. The last meeting I attended of debtors with an assembly of syndicated creditors who were trying to sort out who had which charge on what, who had first rights to which assets, and whether further funds were going to be put up to prop up another decaying piece of the fantasy structure of deal upon deal. The bankers all sighed and were pompous, and the smoky meeting rooms echoed with unspoken 'I told you sos' as the grey hairs with ledgers took over with shaking heads, and the young whiz kids blanched, gulped and realised they would have to behave."

Jonathan said, "You're a contemporary of the whiz kids, but you find yourself as one of the grey hairs, one of the few who were not sucked into the frantic deal-making of the early 70s."

"I've seen shining faces go grey and begin to look unshaven; flamboyant suits with cute waistcoats begin to sag and look unpressed. I've seen honourable men begin to cut corners to save their children's school fees, and wives break down in disbelief. The wives take it worst because the new home with the interior design and the new lifestyle had fed their excitement. The men had deals and then lost the deals, but still have to scheme to survive, have to figure out how to wriggle out of yet another joint and several guarantees, when the several others have gone bankrupt already or disappeared back to California or Brazil or from wherever they had first emerged."

Jonathan said, "But it was the women who helped build the lifestyle of fashion and furniture, and expensive restaurants and expensive schools, and now have to withdraw from it. No heroin addict goes through greater agony. The home that expresses their total personality to the world has to be sold. The Jaguar has to go and be replaced by something called a Ford Escort, justified subsequently by the oil crisis and the need to save fuel for the sake of the economy. But not many of the cutbacks are so easily rationalised."

Nick wondered whether Jonathan was talking from personal family experience.

"Not only that," disclosed Nick, "I've begun to find signs of a dry rot among the crumbling timbers of the rickety structure of loans made by the bank in the heady days of never-ending growth. I suspect that some of the loans I am now sorting out were perhaps made with the connivance and participation of someone in the bank. Maybe someone inside was making it, while someone outside was making it. Perhaps those doling out the large chunks could be seduced by the men they were helping to participate in the lifestyle, having breakfast meetings at the Ritz, followed by weekends at the country house, to eventually participating in the deals."

"No," said Jonathan fiercely, "that's not possible."

"Well, It has definitely happened at some of the smaller secondary banks. I now have a large smell of it emanating from among the piles of files I am sorting and sifting. Each new creditors' meeting brings new disclosures and causes more notes to be added to the bulging briefcase. The paperwork grows bigger as the assets grow smaller. But the smell grows stronger each day."

"We are a large, respectable bank. I am convinced you're fantasising. Do you have any real evidence? Anything that would stand up in court?" Jonathan was almost angrily dismissive.

"Not yet. But I can smell it."

"A smell is not enough for a judge and jury."

But then, just as the stable growth of wealth had begun to crumble, so Nick discovered that his mother was now seriously ill.

CHAPTER 2

Polly

"*Privet dorogoy syn.*" Nick's mother was Russian and they spoke Russian together, but she had never told him how she had come out of Russia during the war. She had never told him anything about the past except how to speak Russian correctly, and Nick, busy with growing up and finding his way, had never questioned her enough to open her up.

Polly Cameron was a small, quiet lady with sadness in her eyes. She smiled easily and took enjoyment in life and in her son, but her face in repose and when unobserved was almost anguished, and she seldom spontaneously initiated the laughter that she could enjoy. Her smallness and her kindness hid her toughness.

When the doctor sent Polly to hospital for checks, Nick went with her, thinking it would be some more prescribed medications for her to take. When the hospital doctor came out, his face told a sad story. He told Nick she would be lucky to survive a year.

His mother who, like property values, had been due to go on forever, now had cancer, and after six months of drug-controlled pain, she died. The painkillers that got her through dimmed her brightness, and in the last few weeks she rambled incoherently and smiled more frequently and naturally than Nick could remember.

Her ramblings were now only in Russian, and on the day before she died, she shocked Nick out of his well-behaved, disciplined acceptance of what was the first real tragedy of his life. The old lady, who had adapted to Britain so well, who loved her English antiques and her English garden, suddenly turned on Nick as on a stranger and cursed him for a British swine, and cursed the English again and again with a wild rage and a bitterness that Nick had never seen before.

The nurse understood nothing and applied another sedative, quietening the storm and diffusing the anger.

Nick lay awake that night, and several other nights, remembering the repeated shouts. "We trusted you, we liked you, and you betrayed us. WHY DID YOU DO IT?! HOW COULD YOU DO IT?!"

She had raised herself and spat at Nick before sinking back, exhausted.

Her illness had gone that frustrating way that cancer deaths can go. A period of confusion, of unexplained back pains, of feeling not right, of taking things easy for a while until things are sorted out. A brave entry into hospital for an exploratory operation followed by the fearful truth, unspoken while there was too much pain, the pain then getting worse, coming home to die with everyone bravely not saying anything.

When it came to speaking the unspoken, she was already very weak. Unable to take her food, how could she be able to say those things that had remained unsaid for thirty years?

As she perhaps summoned up her last reserves for a last confession of the past, of a complete explanation of where they both came from, the doctor had chosen to administer a particularly heavy dose of morphine, or something they had not used before, to enable her to get through the last few days. Along with the centres of pain, the dose cut the threads holding the mind to the present, and from then on she said little that made much sense.

She became softer, pleasanter, but out of touch. She saw figures from the past, called out names Nick didn't know, and relived a life he had never known. She smiled when he came in the room as though she knew he was something good in her life, and she clutched his hand, but her eyes looked over his shoulder at something long gone.

. . • . .

When the funeral was over, Nick went upstairs and started going through her things. He searched for some information. In a long-forgotten cupboard, Nick found a strange old trunk. He managed to open it with great difficulty, and in it he found writings and mementoes and photographs and... a Cossack sword.

Nick started to read her papers and found a painful account of the days at the end of the war. She had never told him about any of this; she had never tried to pass it on. Nick's mother was a Cossack. It must be a joke, he thought. She wasn't a Russian; she was a Cossack.

She was only fifty-seven when she died, and perhaps she had planned to tell him later, much later.

Nick opened a cold bottle of white wine and settled down in front of the fire. The papers were a great jumble, and they appeared to start a long way back. Some were written in Russian and some in English. Some were written at the time of the events they described and were in the form of a diary, whereas others had been written long afterward as a kind of historical record.

Nick tried to arrange them, but it was difficult as the pages were different sizes and the handwriting almost obscure. He opened a newer notebook. The handwriting was English, and it seemed like an historical novel set in 1914 – the earliest year of any of the documents referenced.

But it didn't look like it was written by Polya, his mother. It read as though written by a contemporaneous friend or family member. It was a story about Polya's family ancestors and how they were affected by the war and the development of Bolshevism.

Polya's grandfather, Grishaka, was a farmer in the Don who had fought in the old Turkish wars.

His oldest son Piotra, who was now running the farm, was called up to train to fight in the war in 1914. He had to take his own horse.

The younger son, Gregor, took over running the farm. He and his best friend, Misha Koshevoi, played tricks and chased the prettiest girls, in particular, one called Polya.

A year later, Gregor and his best friend, Misha, were called up. Three months later, they went to the front and fought in the very cruel war. They were Cossacks fighting alongside trained peasants from elsewhere.

Misha Koshevoi became increasingly bitter and agreed with the idea that the war was a personal vendetta of the Tsar and the aristocrats against the Kaiser, and they were just being used as fodder to satisfy his pride.

The Cossacks had a long tradition of serving the Tsar, in return for which they were granted the right to own and work their own lands. The tradition kept them loyal when the conditions of the war and other influences were turning other soldiers away. Bolsheviks were working their way through the regiments and arguing and discussing with all the soldiers over the camp fires.

Misha agreed with the Bolsheviks. Gregor understood the Bolshevik logic, but disliked their methods. He and Misha increasingly went separate ways and, when they did meet, argued fiercely.

Gregor fought and persuaded the Cossack men to be loyal to all their fathers and their customs had stood for. He was awarded the Cross of St. George for his actions in battle.

The war effort collapsed, and the Bolshevik effort gathered strength. Gregor found himself in the same camp as Piotra. They compared notes and opinions and were relieved to find that both were still loyal to their original principles. Misha Koshevoi had disappeared, and Gregor was convinced he had linked up with the Bolsheviks.

The war was over, but so was the Tsar. Piotra and Gregor gathered what supplies they could and made for the Cossack lands where order and sanity still prevailed.

On the return journey, they saw horrific scenes as the newly powerful Reds took summary action to control the situation. They saw officers being killed, and in one town they rode past a row of men hanging in the town square, all well-clothed members of the local community, now grey with twisted faces.

Gregor, whose sympathies were drawn to some of the Bolshevik arguments, was now convinced that the entire enterprise had gone wrong. Piotra had needed no convincing.

Gregor and Piotra returned home to a different village. The remaining villagers had struggled to bring in the harvest.

Their father, Grisha, was older and tired, but proud to have his boys home. He couldn't understand the way the world was being changed by the Bolsheviks.

Polya was away and Gregor heard that Misha had spent time with her when he was home. Misha had told of the collapse of the army and had nothing good to say about Gregor, dismissing his Military Cross as payment for betraying his colleagues. Misha's family were among the poorest in the village. They had embraced the new workers' religion and praised Misha as the man who was to bring justice to the land. Misha Koshevoi had left to join the Bolshevik struggle up North.

Piotra and Gregor tried to work the land and behave as though nothing had changed, but it was hard. A Red army had been formed and was advancing south through the countryside to bring the new form of government to all and establish some control.

The old Cossacks did not want the new form of government. They began to fight back, and an army began to grow. Piotra and Gregor were asked to take a lead, to use the experience of real war to fight the village's battle. A hundred men came forward and offered to fight to maintain their independence. The great Cossack General Krasnov formed an army to fight the Reds. The Hundred, as they became known, were sent off to rousing acclaim.

The fighting lasted for nearly two years. The Reds carried all before them until Krasnov gathered sufficient numbers and fought back.

Gregor was unhappy with the fighting. Neighbour was fighting neighbour, and in some cases friend was fighting friend. Piotra and Gregor went back frequently to help the family, and finally Piotra stayed. Gregor went back to the fighting. On one of his visits home, he heard that Polya was home, and they met up.

Her father did not object to the hurried marriage. Gregor was one of the most respected men among most Cossacks. Even General Krasnov respected his advice.

Polya moved into the Korshunov's hut, and they built an additional room for Gregor's family. When Gregor next returned, he was presented with a rosy daughter who they called little Polya.

(Nick realised this was his mother.)

Before the war ended they all experienced some horrific atrocities, the worst of which were to affect them for the rest of their lives.

The most significant was to finalise their split with the Koshevois forever. Although they had no hand in it, Misha was to never forget, and always believed that they were the ones responsible.

The Koshevois chose to leave Tatarsk once it was clear that the majority opinion within the village was against the Bolsheviks. But they chose to leave just as a disorganised action was taking place between them and the comparative safety of the north. A group of the Bolshevik sympathisers were leaving all together and had made some progress along the road to Kargino when they were surrounded by a gallant troupe of Whites looking for some satisfaction. They were questioned by an arrogant young officer who barely allowed them to explain who they were. He was going to control his mob and let them all proceed when one of his men, who was originally from the village, recognised the Koshevois and denounced them as active Reds. The officer had all twenty lined up by the side of the road and extracted a "confession" out of them by holding a gun against their heads. When the first, a confused old man, refused, the officer pulled the trigger, and the old man fell into the roadside ditch. The others, one by one, admitted to Bolshevism, though with shut eyes and through trembling mouths.

The officer then was at a loss and decided to lock them all up in a small roadside hut. They were crowded in there for several days and nights with no food and water while the Whites argued.

The news had spread about this strange capture and had reached Misha to the North, who was on his way to meet his family, and Gregor to the South, who was trying to turn the unruly gangs of Cossacks into an army. Misha arrived just as the sorry group, which included women and children, were being led out of the hut and lined up by the ditch again. He intervened but only succeeded in being taken and forced to watch as one after another, including his mother and father, were forced to kneel and then shot in the back of the head.

Gregor arrived in time to stop the last few being shot, but not in time to prevent Misha from being beaten viciously and left for dead. Gregor insisted they were needed at a nearby battle, and they found the thought of real fighting more appealing that this unpleasant charade. Gregor led them away and Misha Koshevoi, choking in his own blood, saw him and cursed him, thinking that he was responsible for the whole affair.

White and Cossack soldiery and old-fashioned loyalty were no match for the weight of numbers and dedicated organisation. The Reds crushed the Whites slowly and remorselessly. The Whites had some victories, which they celebrated noisily, but the advance of the Reds continued until they occupied all major towns. Sporadic street fighting continued, and firing squads in back yards hastily finished the work of impromptu courts. Son judged father and brother shot brother. Devotion to ideas and ideals supplanted family feelings. Old Cossacks with a burning passion for the land and for their children were portrayed by the propagandists as cruel despots exploiting the weak and abusing their wives and children. Children devoted to the cause betraying their parents were lauded as heroes.

Misha Koshevoi had returned to the committees up north and his resentment and bitterness festered. He now hated the Korshunovs for more than one reason. He hated Gregor for no longer being his friend, for stealing his girl, for sticking to the bad old ways when he, Misha, had found the glorious new light. But now he hated him for being responsible for the death of his family.

Misha Koshevoi continued to be successful and was appointed the Regional Food Commissar. He was responsible for obtaining food for the Army. His duties included visiting each village and deciding how much grain should be donated by each Cossack. Eventually, once again, he reached his home village.

Gregor had been the most hardworking of all the Cossacks and had been rewarded with the largest harvest. Hearing of the approach of the Food Commissar, the Cossacks had hidden their grain in covered pits and handed over only a small amount. Misha knew where old Grisha kept his reserves and soon unearthed the hide. Gregor was brought before a summary tribunal composed of workers who were only too glad to get their own back. A sentence of death was arrived at rapidly. Misha faced Gregor as he left the court.

The Cossacks revolted, upset that their hardest working member, a war hero with the Military Cross, should be treated in this way. Gregor was freed and Misha escaped, but only just.

Misha was later a success in Moscow and moved steadily up the ladder of committees, groupings and hierarchies. He thrived on intrigue, and the Party liked the way he could be trusted to get things done.

As the Reds consolidated their position within each town and each village, the Korshunovs retrenched and retreated, but they survived. They didn't prosper, but they were not swept away in the bloodbath of revenge that crossed the country.

Piotra and Gregor were still respected for their abilities and their common sense and fairness. When the village voted to form its first Revolutionary Committee, the red peasants were dismayed to see that the two brothers were high on the list and on the governing body. They managed to throw Gregor off, but he was still consulted and respected.

The land was redistributed, and the Korshunovs got less

land each season. Peasants who were not Cossacks or farmers were allowed to farm the land inefficiently.

A decade passed by and the bitterness did not die away but grew with each new humiliation. The Korshunovs and their like were frustrated and torn between intense love for the land and its ways and their hatred for the new regimes that had torn the old ways apart and failed to create something good.

In other villages, there were several horrors. A woman seven months pregnant caught cutting spring wheat was beaten publicly with a plank and died. A mother of three small children who had no husband for he had been arrested, was shot when she was found digging up potatoes at night. Her three children starved to death. The head of another village shot seven people, three of them children, caught plucking grain.

The people in the village all showed signs of starvation, swelling bellies and thin limbs. Brigades searched each home regularly. It was suspicious not to have the signs of starvation.

In 1937, the horror of the Stalin years hit. Unbelievable drama swept through towns, with the NKVD arresting and interrogating hundreds of thousands of people regardless of age, sex, status, rank, or membership of the Party. Fictitious confessions were extracted from terrified party loyalists to inform on other innocent members. Everyone could be in jail, sentenced to ten years in the labour camps, or shot.

The whole nation froze in terror. For a while, it seemed that those in the country could avoid the worst of the horror, but eventually, like cancer, it crept into every home throughout the land. The Korshunovs were lucky and avoided any real attack. The Party was more interested in rooting out its most devoted followers, in tearing down the very tree it had spent years building, than in settling old scores.

Misha Koshevoi was now high up in the NKVD, but he

needed all his talents to survive the enormous power struggle that swept through every organ in the land.

Another section then began, written by Polya:

I grew up in a confused and tortured world. My father was admired and respected by some and reviled by others. I helped on the farm and I did well at school. I met a boy unlike all other boys, and in 1938, at the age of twenty, I married him. My husband, Nikolai Zharkov, is the son of another staunchly anti-Bolshevist family. One year later, as the whole of Europe began to tear itself apart again, I had a son, Alexei.

Nikolai had heard of the old ways from his father who, like Gregor, had been a loyal Cossack and had struggled against the new regime. But he didn't know them. What he did know was what I also knew, and that was the fear and suspicion that we all lived in. The all-pervading influence of the Committees and the Courts that could be used by those willing to toe the Party line to obtain revenge on anyone they pleased.

A classmate at school, who no one liked, was able to use the mechanisms against his own father. Unwilling to work after school to help on the farm, he reported his old father to the Central Village Committee for counter-revolutionary talk and exploitation of labour. His father, a gruff old man who spoke fiercely but had a kind heart, and who grumbled about everything, even the sun when it came out for drying up his soil, and who would have complained about any government out of principle, thought the whole thing a huge joke. But the Committee, who had been waiting for such a chance to take action against a man who seemed to prove that he could farm success-fully, in fact, a good deal more successfully than the members of the Committee, took great delight in fining the old man many roubles and confiscating from him the rights to the good land *that he had farmed for many years.*

The Committees and the Courts were all-powerful. And they appeared always to be manned by the same, by those who talked long and loud about socialist theory, but who did little to get things done. So-called rich peasants, those who had organised their lives and worked hard, were penalised to favour the poor peasants, who were usually too full of cheap vodka to get up to work, but who liked to meet in the barn at night to talk over some more vodka.

Nick groaned and smashed a fist down on the table. Papers flew around the room. He stood up and screamed. He tottered to the window and stared out into the cloudy sky. He stood shaking and shivered in desperation. Eventually, he noticed that the central heating was out, so he lit the gas fire that his mother had always insisted on keeping. He staggered downstairs to make a cup of coffee and dropped the milk in the sink. He sat at the kitchen table and gulped his cup of coffee.

He was shell-shocked. How could she have kept all this from him? She was a Cossack. They had fought against the Bolsheviks.

CHAPTER 3

REVEAL OR
NOT REVEAL?

Nick had been in Spain analyzing the prospects for saving a golf club development which had serious loans from the bank. He had found that some of the loaned funds had moved suspiciously.

When he returned, he had found even more strange movements of funds in other loans. He went back to his office full of uncertainty. Jonathan was doodling and looking out of the window.

"Jonathan, I need your serious advice. I am increasingly uneasy."

"About what? You're admired for doing a very valuable job. Just get on with it."

"I... I... I'm finding more strange movements of funds."

"You're becoming neurotic. Just relax and let the bank get on with its business."

"When I was sent to Spain to see whether that seaside golf club development could be saved, I identified serious shortages of funds in the many bank loans. Funds could have gone either to the man heading the development, or even back to someone in the bank."

"Could have, could have, could have...??"

"That just set me off searching in more depth. I found several companies handling funds that were transferred rapidly to strange overseas locations."

"Strange?"

"To other banks in small overseas islands...."

"Neurotic fantasies, Nick. Just get on with your normal job. That is difficult enough without inventing strange conspiracies. Have you told anyone? Lutz?"

"No. You're the only one I have talked to. Perhaps you're right. I need to concentrate on the actual facts, not on the vague possibilities. But the other thing is...."

Jonathan groaned. "Not more fairy tales?"

"No, these are clear facts. We have been handling large funds from powerful foreigners...."

"What foreigners?"

"Oh, Italians, Germans, Russians..."

"So, what's the problem?"

"Some examples of large funds being transferred into offshore companies that were then used to buy large prime properties in London!"

"Well, probably quite legal. It's their problem, Russia's problem, not ours?"

"Not just Russia. Ukraine also, and Nigeria."

"Oh, my God! Too fantastic! Have you told Lutz?"

"No. I told you. I don't dare. I don't know who is involved."

"Oh! It's beyond me. Too complicated. By the way, are you coming to the reception at the US Embassy?"

"Yes."

Jonathan got up to leave the room. "Perhaps I'll see you there."

CHAPTER 4

THE EMBASSY, 1975

It was at the US Embassy that Nick met both Carmina and Joanne.

Nick stood on the edge of Grosvenor Square and looked across at the big eagle. It looked uncomfortable, unsure whether to crap on the concrete box or take off back to the safety of the mother country. Not that the demonstrations back home were any less abrasive than the one that Nick had read that had surged manically back and forward across the square the evening before, carrying policemen before it and leaving casualties and burnt flags behind. An estimated 15,000 women had taken to the streets to protest against the Government's proposed changes to the 1967 Abortion Act, which could have reduced the circumstances in which women could have an abortion.

Nick pulled his overcoat around him and walked slowly through the square past the statue of Franklin Roosevelt. He wasn't looking forward to the cocktail party but had been told by Lutz that it might be seen in a good light by the visiting Executive Vice President. By which, of course, he meant that his absence would be seen in a bad light. Nick was tired, he had been working long nights, pulling his way slowly through the files that told the story of the past three years. He got a sense of achievement out of piecing together the evidence and resented having to give away this evening.

But he was doubly uncomfortable having knowledge he couldn't share.

He climbed the steps, handed his invitation to one grinning Marine, his coat to another, braced himself and entered the large room, trying hard to appear relaxed and confident at the same time as he searched for a familiar face. He shook hands with a silver-haired, smooth cheeked ambassador-looking man with a stiff hand and loose smile, and a typical kipper tie. Beyond him, along the line, a grizzled, broad-shouldered character crunched his hand and briefly focussed hard grey eyes straight on his when he heard Nick's name.

Across the room, Nick saw Jonathan and steered towards him like a distressed dinghy towards a rescue vessel. He grabbed a glass of something and a small, tasteless, coloured object on the way.

Jonathan was smoothly and imperceptibly dominating a small group of American executives and minor embassy officials, two of whom were girls.

Jonathan folded him into the group and introduced him without failing to complete the end of a story about how comic the matrons of Melbourne were. As the laughter subsided, Jonathan turned around to share the enjoyment and found himself looking into the laughing eyes of a blonde All-American Girl. He quickly looked away and then forced himself to look back and say, "Smooth as champagne, isn't he?" It came out in a hoarse whisper.

She smiled blankly and nodded. She raised her empty glass. "Yes, please." and turned back to listen to the next story. Nick felt himself begin to redden, fought it off and looked around for a waiter.

He found one two groups away, followed him around one

group, finally got two glasses and then looked for the Jonathan group.

He bumped and squeezed his way back, losing most of the cargo on the way. She was alone with Jonathan as he approached, smiling upwards and sipping from a fresh champagne glass.

Nick turned, felt his skin prickle, and stood looking at them from a distance. She was wearing Chelsea boots and was striking, tall, healthy and relaxed. She appeared to be totally absorbed by Jonathan's story, looking straight into his eyes and laughing with him. Nick felt like an intruder. He looked around for another friendly face. He drank one glass, put it down and walked slowly across the room between the groups heading gradually towards the door. He knew that he shouldn't leave too soon, and he must ensure that Lutz saw him before he left. He went to the bar, put his other glass down and picked up another. He didn't like this sort of do. He didn't like the noise; he didn't like the sort of people who came, nor the way they behaved. He was about to turn again to face the buzzing crowd when a laughing voice said, "Well, where's the champagne?"

She was even better looking the second time around, but he classed her as a little rich girl with more charge cards than brains. He handed her a glass. "I'm sorry, you weren't there when I came back."

Nick didn't want her to know that he felt awkward inter-rupting her conversation with Jonathan. She must have seen him because she said, "I've known Jonathan since forever. He's a darling, but as deep as this champagne glass."

She spoke with that East Coast accent that sounded almost British. It reeked of private schools and Cape Cod mansions, and lots of sailing and skiing.

He tried to think of something witty in reply. "Yes. I've always thought that deep down he was really shallow."

"Groucho Marx?" she guessed.

Nick said, "No, someone else. But he looks deep."

"'It is only shallow people who do not judge by appearances.'"

Nick said, "Wilde?"

"Right in one," she said. "You don't look very happy to be here. You look as though you wish you were somewhere else."

Nick said, "I do wish I was somewhere else."

He realised, too late, that he sounded as though he wanted to get away from her. "With you," he corrected clumsily and sounded too forward. "Of course," he corrected again, and grinned foolishly to try to make it all sound jokey, "My name's Nick."

She stared at him. "I'm Joanne. You probably think that mob yesterday has more to commend them than this bunch."

Nick said, "Well, I wouldn't go as far as that. But I would find it hard to pick between them."

"What's wrong with this lot, then? They're all good members of American society." Joanne was challenging now, thrusting out a delicate chin, pouting perfect lips. He had by now sunk the fourth glass and had found very few little canapes to soak up the damage.

"Everyone here is here out of self-interest." Nick waved an arm wildly. "Their main concern is to meet the new influential Ambassador and make sure they get included on the year's invitation lists. The men are here to make contacts to further their business opportunities, and the women are here to make contacts to further their social opportunities. I bet you're dying to meet the Ambassador."

Joanne said, "I have no desire to meet with him right now. But tell me more about this theory. Do you think no one here has an altruistic thought?"

"Well, look at that woman, for example." Nick gestured towards an elegant lady with a shining face and polished hair, who was busy talking, smiling and introducing. "That dress probably cost enough to feed a family for a year, and the jewellery would buy them a house. She has buzzed around the place talking to everyone and is determined not to miss out on a chance."

"I thought you worked for a bank. I think she's the Ambassador's wife and.."

Nick said, "I know. You're going to tell me that she does a lot for charity. She organises events that raise huge sums for starving children, but even the motives behind that are questionable."

Joanne said, "Are motives more important than actions? What are motives worth without actions?" She was brighter than she looked, and Nick was aware that his drink was beginning to talk. "Do you agree with the motives of yesterday's mob?" she asked.

Nick said, "Well, I do. But not with their actions. I think they should be arrested if they cause damage to property, but they are right to protest about the availability of abortion."

There was silence, and Joanne turned slowly away from him and looked around the room. He grabbed another glass and thought he had gone too far. She turned back and said, "You should speak softly if you're going to say things like that in the US Embassy. Shall I tell you a secret?"

He nodded, relieved that she was still with him.

"I was out there yesterday, screaming and shouting."

"In that dress?"

"No. You idiot. It was blue jeans and beads, and I had to run like hell to get away from the pigs." She giggled furiously. "Imagine if they knew."

She was more than pretty interesting.

Nick said, "What are you doing here?"

"God knows. Why did you come?"

He told her.

Joanne said, "Why do we stay?"

Nick said, "You go first."

Joanne said, "No, you go first."

His heart skipped a beat, and then he was breathless. "I have to make sure my boss sees that I am here." They agreed to leave in half an hour and meet in the centre of Grosvenor Square.

Nick saw Lutz across the room, talking intensely with Jonathan. Jonathan was jerking and pointing his finger, making a strong point. Nick hoped they were discussing the football results.

When Jonathan moved away, Nick found Lutz in a corner with the grizzled, broad-shouldered big man. "Nick, I want you to meet Mike Carmina. He's the Cultural Attaché at the Embassy. He spent yesterday taking photographs of the crowd outside as part of his study of British cultural life."

Frank's lips were forced back to show his teeth, and his thick glasses did their best to twinkle. His pale skin was moist. Frank's attempts at humour were forced at the best of times. Carmina was the man least likely to be mistaken for anything cultural in the room, and Frank wanted to show that he knew.

Mike Carmina wasn't smiling. Nick guessed that he didn't smile much. "Bastards, all bastards. We've got their number."

"How many? Two or three hundred?" Nick asked slowly.

Carmina stared at him, "More than that – more like over a thousand – all crazy Commies."

Carmina's hair was the length of a well-used white toothbrush.

"Even the ladies?"

Frank didn't miss cynicism and liked it less. "Mike, Nick is an Englishman who we've had a chance to straighten out. He spent three years at Harvard and then did two years with us in New York." This failed to impress Carmina. For some reason Nick expected him to say that he knew all that.

"Nick is also fluent in Russian. He could help you uncover all the undercover commies in that mob yesterday."

Carmina stood looking silently at Nick. Then he finally said, "Do you get much chance to use the language on the job?"

"No, not at all." Nick looked at Frank.

"Not yet, not yet. Nick's heavily involved in sorting out some of these problem property loans left behind by our old colleagues right here in London." Frank seemed prepared to forget that he had been around just as much as his old colleagues, who had now run for cover.

"Not much call for Russian in that line of work. But the new business now is syndicated Eurocurrency loans, and quite a few of these are to Eastern bloc countries, so we may be using some of his linguistic talents soon."

This was news to Nick, and since it was most unlikely that he should leave the problem loans department just when he was getting near the end, he just looked blankly at Frank.

"Well," said Frank, appearing to read his scepticism, "it may be something you can do on a part time basis as the peak of your current work runs down."

"Perhaps we should have a talk sometime," said Carmina.

"Anytime, anytime. Although I hardly think that I...."

"Oh, we all have to play our part. Even I..." Frank's voice faded away as Carmina spotted someone over his shoulder, raised his hand as if in apology, and sidled out of the group.

Nick looked into his glass and asked, "Is he really...?"

"Well," said Frank stiffly, trying to correct his indiscretion. "If he is, we don't know about it." Frank looked around the room while talking to Nick, clearly feeling that he was missing out on talking to someone more worthwhile.

"Where's the E.V.P., Frank?"

"Over there, by the window, he's talking to the Ambassador's wife and daughter." Nick looked across the room and saw the Executive Vice President, Frank's boss from New York, a bulky man with silver hair and very white teeth in a permanent smile, smiling and nodding at the very talkative American lady in the expensive couturier dress with the polished face and glossy hair. Nick felt his face redden with embarrassment as he gradually realised through the crowds who the young girl with them was.

"That's the Ambassador's daughter?"

"Yes, Joanne Kavanagh. Quite a doll, isn't she? I bet she costs the old man a packet. But he can afford it. You know that he..." And Frank launched into one of his favourite topics, the retelling of how rich men had become rich. He told the story, which Nick knew because he had read it in *Time* the month before when the Ambassador had been appointed.

Peter Kavanagh, the Ambassador, had built his fortune against all odds in the thirties, multiplied it as a patriot through the war, and consolidated and achieved respectability in the fifties and sixties. Now, as an extremely wealthy and influential member of the American establishment, he was achieving the ultimate recognition, the equivalent of a title in Britain. Nick secretly believed that all American billionaires, regardless of industry, had made their pile through bootlegging, extortion, or exploitation.

"Come on, I'll introduce you to the E.V.P." Nick agreed, hoping to embarrass her.

She saw them coming through the crowd and grinned at him. She kept grinning through the introductions.

Later, at the restaurant, Joanne challenged, "People behave differently when they know I'm the Ambassador's daughter. I bet you wouldn't have tried out those wet left-wing ideas if you'd known who I was."

Nick said, "You're right, probably not. Do you mean you don't agree with them?"

Joanne said, "I don't know. I can see both sides."

Nick countered, "If you're not part of the solution, you're part of the problem...."

"Say, who's doing the talking? How do you reconcile your opinions with your position at the bank?"

"There's no conflict. I just don't express my opinions too strongly to the wrong people."

Joanne said, "Sounds like a cop out to me."

"Maybe I'm hedging my bets until I mature into a right-wing property owner. Or until the Unions finally take over the running of the banks. One or the other. What about you?"

"Also, you wouldn't have made a pass at me."

"Did I make a pass at you? I thought the ball was on the other foot."

It was late, and Nick wondered if she was going to slow down. "Don't you go to Annabel's for breakfast at this time?"

Joanne laughed scornfully. "My friends do. I can't stand that junk."

"I heard Jonathan ask Frank if he'd like to go there. Frank got over-excited."

"What do you want to do?" she asked, looking him straight in the eyes.

Nick said, "You go first."

"No, you go first."

He hesitated and then said naturally, "You know what I want to do."

She wasn't going to let him get away with it. "And what's that?"

"The same as you want to do."

Joanne went very silent and looked at the table.

After a while he asked, "I haven't jumped the gun, have I?"

She looked up at him and said very seriously, "No, I don't believe you have. But I think we should wait a little. Maybe until we've got the formality of a couple of dates out of the way."

Much later, Nick woke in bed and remembered that Carmina had not asked him where and why he had learned his Russian, which everyone always did. Probably had a file on him.

And no one at the event had mentioned Nixon's behaviour or problems. But then, no one was celebrating the fact that the UK had a Labour government under Harold Wilson. The Tories had won the popular vote, but Labour took more seats but not a majority, and the Tories failed to form a coalition with the Liberals.

CHAPTER 5

THE OLD COSSACK, 1975

Nick knew that his mother had visited an old man in Bayswater. Someone from the old days, she said once, although never again. She usually pretended that there had been no old days.

"Never look back," she said. "The past is not a good place to build your future."

Peter, that was his name. But Peter what? That evening, Nick poured himself a glass of cold Chardonnay and worked his way through his mother's large battered address book. He found no Peters. The likeliest was a Frolov, Pyotr with a number that looked like a Bayswater one.

He dialled the number. An old voice with a heavy Russian accent answered, "Yes, this Frolov. Who is that?"

"Mr. Frolov, this is Nicholas Cameron, Mrs. Polly Cameron's son."

There was a lengthy silence, then, "Who is that?"

"Nicholas Cameron. I think you knew my mother, Mrs. Cameron?"

"No," said the old voice, fading away, "I'm sorry..."

"Polya Zharkov, perhaps you knew her as Polya Zharkov."

Nick was mouthing his words in a parody of an English learner. Then he remembered to speak Russian, "Moya mama Polya."

The old voice immediately sounded sharper, more confident in Russian. Of course he knew Polya. How was she? He hadn't seen her for some time now; she had neglected him. When he heard the news, Nick could tell he was very upset and found it hard to speak.

"I would like to come to see you, if I may?" Nick asked.

"Of course, of course." And he gave him the address and careful directions to ring the bell marked Fellows.

The house was a tall Victorian in Sussex Gardens with a pillared portico and flanked by scruffy Bed and Breakfast hotels. It needed fresh paint and a few repairs. Nick went up the steps and found the bell marked Fellows; the top one of six. He rang it several times before he heard a wheezing and shuffling come to the door.

Pyotr Frolov was a bent, grizzled, and angry-looking man. It turned out that the look of anger was caused by his being out of breath.

"I am afraid," he wheezed after they had shaken hands and introduced each other, "that I live on the top floor. You must take a deep breath."

"Oh, I'll make it alright, but it must be hard for you; you should get the landlord to give you a lower floor."

"He never do that. He too mean," and he chuckled wheezily, "You see, I am landlord, and better rents for lower floors. Anyway, good view upstairs, and exercise good for old heart."

Nick looked round the small flat and saw the old worn but comfortable furniture of a man who cared little for appearances but liked the things he knew around him. He saw a black and white photo in a silver frame of a young couple with their arms around each other, their faces beaming, their hair blowing in the wind, their eyes squinting in the sun. He saw objects in the room and on the walls that were not English. Incongruously, a battered grey filing cabinet stood in one corner. The room was dark and Nick could see the lights of other houses. He sat in a heavy collapsing sofa and took a small glass of vodka off the tray.

"To your mother, to my darling Polly." Nick could see that the old man was crying softly. They drank and Nick sat, embarrassed, not knowing where to begin.

He cautiously told the old man about her death.

"I wish you call me," Frolov said sadly.

"I didn't know. And she... she. Well, I suppose she never really knew until it was too late..." he found it difficult to talk about the death.

The old man sensed his difficulty and asked, "Your Russian is very good. Did you always speak it together?"

"Yes. That is when no one else was around. She didn't like people knowing she was Russian. Not that she was ashamed, just that she didn't seem to want to talk about it, somehow."

"She never told you about the old days, did she?"

Nick shook his head, "No. Never. It was only afterwards that I found some papers. And when she was dying, you know, not really knowing what she was saying, she said something strange."

"What was that?"

"She seemed to be angry. She was accusing... me... the British. She said she had been betrayed." Then, after a pause, "She had never said that before."

"You know, Nikolai, people who go through a terrible experience, like the war, either never stop talking about it, like me, and become known as bores to be avoided, or they bottle it up to forget, like your mother. She didn't want to spend her life remembering. She wanted to build something new."

Nick said, "And the past is not a good place to build the future...."

"Yes, she used to say that to me. She thought I was an old fool, always living in the past, always wanting to talk over the old days."

"Tell me about them."

"She told you nothing?" Frolov asked the question a second time.

"She told me nothing when she was alive."

"But she left something written?"

Nick told him about the bundles of scribbled pages with the unfinished history.

Frolov said, "Well, so she wrote a lot. She never told me that she had done so much writing. It was her way of talking, I suppose. There were two great unmentionables in her life, and perhaps she managed to write about them."

"Two great unmentionables?"

Frolov became vague then and asked what Nick had read.

Nick told him about his mother being a Cossack and about the Korshunovs in the First World War and the start of the Revolution.

"I, too, am a Cossack. Perhaps the last of the Cossacks." He laughed at the incongruity of it.

"Why the last? Surely there are many still left in Russia – Cossack dance troops, circus performers...."

"Those are not Cossacks! They are a parody of the real Cossacks. No, the Cossacks were destroyed by the Russian peasants."

"Destroyed? When, why, how?"

"The Cossacks started the first opposition to the Revolution. Not, as the historians think, because they were the traditional supporters of the Tsar, his personal army on occasion, but because they were fiercely independent of all authority."

"What exactly is a Cossack? Most people think it's a soldier with a fur hat, cape, boots and a big moustache who rides like a wild man and dances like a mad one! I know it's not, but who exactly are they?"

"That is a good question, and one that is not asked. The Cossacks were farmers first. Soldiers second. They farmed fertile lands in the south of Russia. In the northeast corner of the Black Sea is the Sea of Azov, which lies to the east of the Crimea.

Into the corner of the Sea of Azov flows the river Don. The Don starts to the north and flows through flat fertile lands to the large towns of Novocherkassk and then Rostov-on-Don. On either bank were the villages and farms of the Don Cossacks."

"What made them soldiers?"

"Well, originally, they were not farmers. They were migrants and mercenaries. The Russian princes hired Cossacks to fight the Turkic-Tatars, Bashkirs, Kirghiz and Mongols. The Russian Cossacks were created, and a tradition of service to the Russian Tsar was established. It continued for four hundred years."

"But they became farmers?"

"Yes, they were migrants who fought, became farmers, and then became real soldiers."

"You know a lot about Cossack history."

"But what has it to do with your mother? Not very much, I suppose, but you asked about the origin... I can be a bore on these matters. Also, it will help you understand the significance of the Cossacks to the Bolsheviks at the time of the Revolution and later.

"Throughout the centuries, there has been a relationship of love and hate between the tsars, or Moscow, and the Cossacks. Moscow has needed and feared the Cossacks, but has not wanted to grant them the land and freedom that they promised. But the Don Cossacks were beginning to settle. They established thirty stanitsas, villages, on the Don. These increased to about 125. No agriculture yet, so they lived from trapping, hunting, fishing, some salt farming, some cattle and stock raising and from war, raiding and looting other communities."

"A pretty frightening bunch. A military bunch."

"Military. But they had a democracy. The ataman or chief, and his deputy, esaul, elected by the popular assembly that met in Cherkessk."

The old man poured another glass of vodka for Nick, who sipped it slowly and decided to keep quiet and let the old Cossack run and run.

"The old prohibitions on agriculture 'under penalty of death' had gone, and the Cossacks became farmers. Pasturelands were allocated according to position and influence. The rich began to acquire lands and build up fairly large and wealthy farms. In this way, the Don Cossacks became an exclusive class."

"Never an aristocracy. Still simple fighting and farming men. They liked to dress extravagantly but with little finery. They wore loose trousers and leather knee boots and carried the nagaika, a flail whip."

Nick was desperately curious. "But what happened in the last war? Did you know my mother was married and had another son? I think I have a brother still in Russia? And how was my mother affected by the ending of the war? Do you know what happened?"

The old man looked sad. " I know some things. I will tell you what I know."

CHAPTER 6

JOANNE AGAIN

Nick met with Joanne again. They had an intimate dinner.

When he looked at Joanne, Nick felt very close to her. So close that he now felt he had someone he could share his many concerns with.

Joanne said, "Relax, Nick, relax. This should be a fun time. I know our relationship is still slightly undercover, but there is nothing we have done to be ashamed of."

Nick nodded, but still felt awkward.

Joanne said, "We can be open if we want to?"

Nick shook his head. "I know, I know. But it's not just that. I have a number of strange findings that are very concerning. No, not about us."

"About what, then?"

Nick hesitated. "About... my mother's history. And about things going on at the bank?"

"What? Tell me."

Nick said, "But I don't want to waste your time. We want to be together...."

"And to share things...? If you have any problems, any issues,

I would like to help you resolve them. What's concerning about your mother's history?"

"Well, you know she died a few months ago? I told you she was Russian, and we spoke Russian?"

"Yes?"

"Well, I knew little of her history, of her family, of her background."

"Yes?"

"Well, I have found a load of papers, of notes in diaries uncovering a great deal."

"And what does it tell you?"

"A strange Cossack history.... My mother was a Cossack."

"What?"

Nick tried to give a simplified version of the early history.

"The Cossacks were against the Bolshevik revolution. They fought the Bolsheviks. Against the Communists."

Joanne gasped, "That's a surprise."

"As the war began, the Cossacks wanted the Germans to invade and fight the Communists."

"What a story! But why was she in England?"

"She married a Scottish doctor at the end of the war – Dr. Cameron."

"Your father?"

"Yes, but he's no longer alive. I'm still learning the truth. I have some of the diary entries with me. Can I share them with you?"

"Yes. Please read."

They went back to Nick's flat, and he began to read.

"I found, hidden in the back of a drawer in a desk, a carefully written, and even more carefully hidden, diary. Mother had written a complete history lesson. A very personal history lesson. And she never told me."

Nick read aloud something he had not yet read.

"When the Germans came a second time, we were glad. We didn't like them and we didn't like their methods, but we were glad they came. For the first time since the civil war, we had hope that we could overthrow the Bolsheviks, the Communist Party. For the first time it looked as though we could get our lands back. We were not well read, we had no newspapers with international news, no wirelesses with which to listen to the BBC Overseas service. And even if we had read The Times during the thirties, we would not have known what the Germans were really like.

What we did know, and know so well that our hearts bled, was that our current government was an evil one, and one that we would do anything to remove. We would make a pact with the Devil. We did not know if we could, in that way, remove the Devil we knew.

The Germans invaded Russia in 1942. They had remarkable success. Their armies swept triumphantly across Russia to Leningrad, and the story there is relatively well known. What is less well known is that in the south they advanced several thousand miles across the Ukraine right up to Cossack territory and right across to the Ural Sea. They met with little opposition and, in fact, were received in some territories like an army of liberation.

I had married in 1938 to a brave man called Nikolai. A year later we had a son, and we called him Alexei. He was the love of my life, and for a year nothing else mattered to me."

Nick stopped reading, as he was once again shocked. His mother had a first husband. And she had named Nick after her first husband. And he had, or still had, a brother called Alexei Zharkov. Where was he now, Nick wondered? Where were any of them now?

Nick carried on reading:

"But then the war drew near and my father, Gregor Korshunov, heard that the Cossack Generals were returning from abroad. Finally, the news came that Krasnov himself was coming back, and then that he was forming a Cossack Regiment to fight alongside the Germans to take the war up North, retake Moscow and drive the Communists out forever. The dream was an old one, twenty years old, but it gripped my father like passion, and when the call came from Krasnov, he knew he had to go."

Joanna gasped and grabbed his arm to stop him reading. "This is overwhelming. You Cossacks fought with the Germans against the Bolshevik–communist government?"

Nick slowly nodded his astonished head. "I can't read any more."

Joanna persevered. "And you have a brother! A half-brother? In Russia? ... Were you aware?"

"It is completely new information."

Joanna nodded with understanding. They sat staring at each other. Both of them overwhelmed.

Joanna tried to change the subject. "And what about your worries at the bank? They must now seem trivial?"

Nick turned and looked bewildered. "No, no, not trivial. Definitely not trivial. But very different."

"What is it?" Joanne almost smiled.

Nick started cautiously, "I have suspicions... Suspicions that someone is dipping their hands into the till..."

"Someone? Who?"

"I... I don't know."

"Have you told anyone? Accused anyone?"

"No, not yet. I'm not sure enough. The only person I've discussed it with is... Jonathan..."

"Jonathan??! And what does he say?"

"I don't think he wants to know anything about it. I think he would rather be kept out of the uncertain wondering." Nick was doubly puzzled. "I should not have told you about my suspicions. I have no evidence. Yet."

"I'll carry on reading if I may."

"For Nikolai, it was different. He had heard of the old ways from his father who, like Gregor, had been a loyal Cossack and had struggled against the new regime. But he didn't know them. What he did know was what I also knew, and that was the fear and suspicion that we all lived in. The all-pervading influence of the Committees and the Courts that could be used by those willing to toe the Party line to obtain revenge on anyone they pleased.

A classmate at school, who no one liked, was able to use the mechanisms against his own father. Unwilling to work after school to help on the farm, he reported his old father to the Central Village Committee for counter-revolutionary talk and exploitation of labour. His father, a gruff old man who spoke fiercely but had a kind heart, and who grumbled about everything, even the sun when it came out for drying up his soil, and who would have complained about any government out of principle, thought the whole thing a huge joke. But the Committee, who had been waiting for such a chance to take action against a man who seemed to prove that he could farm successfully, in fact, a good deal more successfully than the members of the Committee, took great delight in fining the old man many roubles and confiscating from him the rights to the good land that he had farmed for many years.

The Committees and the Courts were all-powerful. And they appeared always to be manned by the same, by those who talked long and loud about socialist theory, but who did little to get things done. So-called rich peasants, those who had organised their lives and worked hard, were penalised to favour the poor peasants, who were usually too full of cheap vodka to get up to work, but who liked to meet in the barn at night to talk over some more vodka.

So when the Germans came in 1942, and the call came to join the new Cossack army, there was no shortage of volunteers. The old men pulled out their old uniforms and their old saddles and equipment. The young men leaped on their horses and showed off like crazy. We were all aware that the methods of war had changed, but the Germans were going to equip and train us.

The Cossack army marched away in glory but was never used in a real battle. The Germans never really trusted us, and so they lost battles that we could have won for ourselves.

As the Germans retreated, the Cossack army retreated with it westwards, away from the Cossack lands. I left the village and followed the army. I not only did the chores that were expected of a camp follower, but I trained as a soldier and learned to use the weapons the Germans reluctantly allowed us to have.

Little Alexei was only four and was a beautiful boy. He was dark and quick like his father, had fierce eyebrows and was full of mischief. I cry when I think about him. I left him in good hands because my uncle Piotra stayed behind, and he and his wife loved him almost as much as their own grandchildren. When we left, we thought it would only be for a short time, that we would be back, triumphant. Those who had fought in the Cossack army could not stay, and so many wives and families moved out with the army as it went.

I could have taken Alexei with me, but it would have been difficult, and I decided it would not have been fair. Even now I do not know whether I made the right decision. Would he have survived all that we later went through? I don't know. Would he have preferred to live here than there, supposing he had survived? I don't know that either. Has he had a good life? What is he doing? Does he know I exist? I don't know. I don't know."

Silence. Then Joanna said, emotionally, "How upsetting for your mother."

Nick gritted his teeth. "I have to know. I have to know. Has he survived? Where is he?"

Joanna held Nick. "I understand now. Your strange findings. Your emotional problems and issues. I will help you resolve them. I will help you find a way. You are important to me, and getting your answers is more than important."

They hugged. And Nick knew that he had found a soulmate.

CHAPTER 7

NICK HAD TO KNOW

Nick had to know.

Frolov knew some things. "I know where she came from, I know who she married in Russia, I know she left a son behind, I know her father-in-law and her husband fought against the Russians on the side of the Germans and that she was there. But I don't understand why and I don't know what happened after that."

Frolov himself was puzzled. "But she didn't explain it. Some things you cannot explain. Your life is dedicated to fighting what you think is the world's greatest evil. Along comes someone else who is prepared to fight that evil, and so you join forces. You don't know that the rest of the world thinks that the second evil is worse than the first until afterwards. You don't have *The Times* to read every day to tell you what to think. And if you had followed *The Times* before the war, you would still have been wrong." He was angry, and he rose to walk up and down, panting and wheezing.

"Do you know that *The Times* suppressed their correspondents' cables from Germany analysing Hitler's plans in 1937? Geoffrey Dawson, the stupid editor, wrote the following to his

Berlin correspondent when he heard that the Nazi top brass was criticising *The Times*." Frolov picked up an old newspaper cutting out of a battered box file, and he read. "It would interest me greatly to know precisely what it is in *The Times* that has produced this antagonism in Germany. I did my utmost to keep out of the paper anything that might hurt their susceptibilities."

"What was worse," he asked Nick, "to use the help of the Germans to fight the evil of Communism or to use the help of the Russians to fight the evil of Nazism?"

He didn't expect an answer. "Perhaps we should judge it on the numbers that each side killed. The Nazis, we are told, killed some six million innocent civilians. Stalin alone accounted for over ten million, and many are still in camps or unaccounted for. Tell me – which is the greater evil?"

He went out of the room to make some tea, and Nick sat and looked at the picture of the happy couple in the dim light.

The old man brought in an old battered silver tray with a large teapot covered in a large old tea cosy and two large chipped cups. He poured the tea and started on his story without delay.

"By the end of the war, there were over thirty thousand Russians in three regiments fighting or ready to fight the Red Army. To call them Russian was an unfair simplification. They were made up of practically every nationality except Russian: Ukrainians, Lithuanians, Cossacks, Croats, in fact, every nationality that didn't want to be ruled by the Russians. They were all deserters from the Soviet Army, or prisoners who turned.

On top of that we had the White Russian Armies that had reformed and regrouped when the war began. Old White Russian generals, like General Karpov, had come out of their lairs in Paris and Vienna, and had returned to their old stamping grounds as the German advance drove right into the south of the Soviet Republic right up to the Black Sea and beyond to the Caspian. They reformed their old armies and the local people came flocking to them. Or some of them did.

The trouble was that the German High Command could never decide how much to trust these White Armies and never gave them enough arms and ammunition, and never really allowed them to get on with the fighting, and they would probably have done better than the Germans. After all, they knew the country better, they knew the enemy better, and they had the motivation, which was to recapture their homeland from the barbarism of Bolshevism.

"I know something about this," said Nick quietly.

"How can you? You're too young. You were not there."

"I know something of this," Nick muttered, shaking his head. "My mother...I read..."

"You can't know."

The old man took a long look at Nick and sighed again. "As the German army began to retreat out of the Ukraine, the White Russian regiments retreated with them. One was composed mainly of Ukrainians, and another a Cossack horde. The Cossacks retreated to Poland and formed a Cossack village there. But they were allowed to do little fighting, and as the Russian Army advanced, they were ordered to pull back and trek right across Germany, through Austria down into Italy. This was not just an army of soldiers but a full encampment with women and children carrying baggage, household goods and even furniture on carts.

"The Cossacks have always lived by the horse and the sword, and when their nation moved, it moved by horse. The logistics were horrific, and the chaos they caused and left behind was dreadful. They were not popular wherever they went, but they had little choice.

"As the war drew to an end, they found themselves in Northern Italy, in the Dolomites."

"In Tolmezzo," whispered Nick.

"Yes, in Tolmezzo," the old man looked quizzically at Nick. "So, you do know something about this."

"Only some things... I need to know more."

CHAPTER 8

CIA RECRUITMENT, 1975

Nick didn't like Mike Carmina. He was the sort of American who still thought the USA was the greatest power in the world, and who thought the only reason they hadn't swept away the Vietcong was that a liberal Congress had held the all-powerful military back. He couldn't face up to the truth that the Vietnamese war was a wrong cause, and a lost cause.

He was surprised when Carmina rang him and asked him out to lunch. After the short conversation they'd had at the Embassy, they had met one more time in Frank's office. Nick had just returned from his trip to Mexico and had gone into his boss' office to tell him about his suspicions with regard to the siphoning off of the funds.

"Nick. You remember Mike Carmina, don't you? He's just come to look through my filing cabinet."

Carmina was sitting on the long sofa that V.P.s were allowed in their offices. He got up with a very big grin and enveloped Nick's hand in his massive one. "Hey, how are you? Still wasting your Russian?" He sat down again and leaned back as though appraising Nick carefully.

"Yes, still wasting it, but I've just been misusing some of my Spanish."

"Oh, yeah. Where was that?"

"Mexico. I've just been to Mexico, helping to tidy up one of the syndicated loans we've just completed."

Carmina showed interest, although it was nothing to do with him. "What was the loan for?"

"It was a project loan for the sugar industry. Mexico has the third largest sugar industry in the world, and it's currently going bust."

"So you're lending them money. That sounds a swell idea." Carmina laughed. "Why are they going bust?"

"Three reasons. The world price is at an all-time low, so they're exporting at no profit. Their equipment is all out of date since the industry was built up in the early part of the century, so their costs are high and their labour content is far too high. But the main reason is that the domestic price hasn't been raised for ten years."

"Why not?"

"Because sugar is an important component of the cost of living index, and they want to keep inflation down, but principally because sugar is an emotional product and industry. It was in the sugar plantations that the Revolution with Zapata and so on started. And they are still owned by very rich families and worked by very poor cane cutters and labourers."

"What, still?"

"Yes, still. You should see the style in which these families still live. Huge estancias with beautiful old colonial houses, masses of servants, private planes – I was flown round in one – the famous Revolution never really changed things all that much."

Carmina was almost bored. "So why keep the price down now?"

"By keeping the price down, the Government forces the sugar plantations to go bust, the owners come to the Government for funds to keep going, the Government lends them the money to keep going, and the following harvest, when they can't pay it back, they reluctantly take them over."

"Back door nationalisation?"

"Precisely. A third of the Sugar mills now belong to NAFIN-SA, the State industrial holding company, and the remainder soon will."

"A sort of Industrial Reorganisation Company? You sound as though you approve?"

Nick stumbled on with his explanation. "I have no sympathy for the old sugar mill owners who lived like kings, took all they could, exploited the poorly paid workers, and put nothing back. I think a State combine of sugar mills will be able to modernise, plant new faster growing, better yielding strains, invest in modern cane cutting machinery, and rebuild the old mills. The industry will be rebuilt and will provide a source of new employment and export growth."

"But?"

"Well, it's the corruption. The place is shot through with it."

Frank jumped in, "Something you've got to live with in the third world. Nick, as long as we are not part of it, it's not something we can eliminate, so if we don't do the business, some other bank will. And remember, it's all a sovereign risk; the country itself guarantees the loan, so if something goes wrong, we can't lose."

"Yes, I know all that, and it's not just personal distaste for the way business is done out there, but I'm uncomfortable...." Nick hesitated.

He stopped and looked at Frank. "This is possibly something we should talk about privately."

"Don't worry about Mike. Who better to talk to about corruption? He may even be able to give us a hand."

Nick was getting uncomfortable. "Well, the fact is, I'm not sure that the bank isn't involved in some way."

"What do you mean?" Frank's voice had just got serious; he rose from his chair and came round and sat in the chair facing the sofa. Nick suddenly felt very nervous.

"Well, of the 250 million dollars that were lent to NAFINSA by the syndication of twenty banks, some three percent, or about seven and a half million, were paid out in syndication and management fees back to the banks."

"Yes."

"Well, that leaves some 242 and a half million, and I could only trace 150 million as ever having been invested in the sugar industry."

"So someone skimmed a little off the top."

"Just a little."

Carmina leaned even further back and gave a long, low whistle. "That I understand. I'm not sure I caught much of the rest, but ninety-two million missing, I think, is what they call grand larceny."

"Why do you think the bank is involved?" Frank's voice was icy, his thick glasses glittered.

"We are the managers. There is no way, given the route all the funds take, and given the authorities needed, that much could have been siphoned off without the complicity of someone here in the Bank."

"How come you stumbled on this? You were sent out to make arrangements for the next quarter's interest and capital repayments, not to look into the past."

"They invited me out to the old San Pedro mill. We flew out there on a glorious day, landed at the mill's private air base, and had a huge asado, that's a barbecue, on the grounds of the lovely rambling old house, and then flew back to Mexico City before night fell. When everyone was sleeping off the effects of the lunch and the wine, I asked the assistant manager to show me around the mill. I was hoping to see the vast new investments that had been poured into the plant and machinery according to the project plan we had published in our prospectus. The refurbishment of San Pedro was a key feature in the new investment plan."

"And what did you find?"

"I found a museum. I found a sugar mill that had been built sixty years ago and had been kept going by brilliant engineers with enthusiasm and homemade parts. A lot of love had gone into that mill, but no new investment."

The two men were very silent.

"When I got back, I didn't say anything to anyone. I thought I had better report back to you first. I got friendly with one of the young accountants back at the office, and we went round drinking in the Zona Rosa one evening. He drank Bloody Marys, and I managed to persuade the barman to leave the vodka out of mine. At two in the morning, he told me that the grand total of funds invested was just over one hundred and fifty million. He didn't know what had happened to the balance. He was bitter. He said, 'You know what this country is like. Everyone gets their hands in the till.' I think you could get some information out of him."

Frank went to the window and looked at the traffic in Moorgate. Carmina appeared to take charge of the meeting.

"I'll look into this for you, Frank. Don't you say a word of this to anyone, Nick. We don't want the people responsible warned. What's the name of this guy in Mexico? I can probably get one of our guys in Mexico to talk with him."

"Emilio Sanchez."

Nick hadn't been sent back to Mexico, and Frank had said it was better if they did not talk about the problem there, but that, "Mike is on top of things."

Nick wondered whether it was usual for US Government agents to look into the possibility of fraud within a bank, and then remembered the foreign country implications, and it seemed the most reasonable thing to do.

"What about the Paradiso Club business? Do you think that is connected?"

Nick had reported his suspicions on the missing Paradiso Club de Golf to Frank, and to his relief had been taken off the account. Frank had said he was handing it over to the Internal Audit Department.

"I hadn't thought of that. It could be. Anyway, Mike is taking a look at that as well."

Nick was surprised. The Paradiso fraud was not something one would normally get a CIA man involved in.

"What else have we found out there?"

"Well, it looks as though you may have exaggerated a little…" then seeing Nick's look of exasperation, "but of course, we can't afford to ignore any suspicion of theft, even though we are talking about considerably less than the Mexico business. Once again, Nick, I can't emphasise enough the importance of not mentioning a word to any other party. To no one. You talk about this to no one. For your own sake as much as anything else."

· · • · ·

Now Carmina was asking Nick out to lunch. They went to the City Boot, an old wine cellar of dark wood panels, racks of dusty wine bottles, and ancient Cockney waitresses that Mike found "had real old charm." Nick wondered how it had found its way onto the second floor of one of that row of sixties glass boxes that now made up London Wall.

Carmina ordered a steak very rare and a Coke. Nick watched him cut off a large lump, change the fork to his right hand, stab the bleeding meat and wave it angrily. He went on about the soft Labour Government and the mess it was getting Britain into.

Nick was wondering whether he could ask him about the Mexican puzzle when Carmina suddenly changed tack. "Nick, I think I can help you."

"How's that?"

"I was talking with Jonathan the other day. He was telling me some of your background."

Nick felt a sudden fury. What the hell was Jonathan doing telling a man like Carmina his private life? Carmina noticed immediately. "He just thought maybe I could help you. And I think I can."

Nick looked across the phony restaurant and remembered that it was Carmina's job to find things out about people. "You know, it's my job, asking people about other people."

"Why should you want to help me?" Nick asked coldly.

"Well, I have to admit that my motivation is not exactly totally altruistic."

"And what is your motivation? Is it exactly totally self-interested?"

"Hey, Nick. Calm down. I'm only some poor sucker who might be able to give you a hand and get a favour in return." He grinned broadly with a row of perfect white teeth sharpened on many sides of rare beef.

Nick took hold of himself and asked quietly, "OK, what's the story?"

"Jonathan tells me you're trying to find a long-lost brother in Russia. Is that right?"

"Half-brother. That's right. But I haven't even tried so far."

"Well, let me have a try for you."

"I don't get it. I thought you were..."

"You're right. I am. But we're not just plotting assassinations and photographing secret documents all day long. We also have extensive contacts with each other for all sorts of purposes. And through these contacts we can probably get the information you're wanting much faster than you can. Going through the correct channels in Russia takes three times as long as the indirect."

"Like Mexico. Only in Mexico, it takes ten times as long."

Carmina ignored Nick's reference to Mexico.

"So I think I may be able to find your brother."

"Well, it may be worth a try. You don't think it may be counterproductive?"

"What do you mean?"

"That the Russians will take a special interest in someone in whom the CIA is interested?"

"They won't know. We have contacts within working for us all the time. They'll get the information for us, supposing it is obtainable."

"Isn't that rather a waste of resources?"

"Here's where we come to the self-interest. We think maybe you can do us a favour. We have a shortage of good couriers for material in Russia. And if you were to be making trips to Russia, then perhaps you could carry some material for us."

"What, through customs?"

"No. We have no difficulty getting stuff in and out. It's delivering material once it's in that's not so easy."

"Delivering it where?"

"To our contacts. Usually they're ordinary folk living in small apartments in boring blocks on the outskirts of Moscow. But we have a shortage of men who are unknown to the KGB and who can travel without being spotted. And who can speak Russian."

"But why should I be travelling to Russia?"

"I've had a word with Frank, and he now thinks that this might be a good time for you to further your career by using your language skills more fully by participating in the team that's helping to negotiate the forthcoming multi-million dollar syndicated Russian loan."

Nick looked down at the table and tried to think. To see his brother, and to see Russia, to see where his mother and his grandfather had grown up and fought their battles.

"I may not be a desirable visitor to the USSR."

"Because of your mother's background? No problem. Once you become a citizen of a foreign country they don't care. Remember that our Security Advisor is of Russian extraction, and at least two of your Cabinet Ministers have parents from the Baltic states."

Nick was very excited, more excited than he had been since his mother died. He found it hard to get over her death and thought about her every day, and felt the useless guilt that survivors do. Visiting Russia and finding his half-brother would help pay back some of the debt he felt.

· · • · ·

The next time they met, Carmina had the information.

"Your brother is living in Rostov. Rostov-on-Don. It is a large port on the Sea of Azov, just north east of the Black Sea."

Nick was partially surprised. "Cossack country."

"Yes, that's where they all are."

"Were."

Carmina questioned, "What do you mean?"

"Were. That's where they all were. They are no longer there. They were all driven out or destroyed."

"I don't know what you mean. Anyway, your brother is there. He works in the docks as some kind of supervisor. Now that you know who and where he is, you should make a formal application to visit him."

Nick was puzzled. "So now I must rely on the correct channels?"

"I'm afraid so. It might be counterproductive if we were to make the application. But we will help you apply correctly. Go for it. It will be exciting. Get a life." He chuckled and seemed more relaxed than usual. "I hear you're in line to join the team on the Russian loan."

"I've started work on it already. In fact, I've been taken off everything else, which is a bit disappointing."

"You don't need to worry. We have our tabs on those potential problems you uncovered. Looks as though there may have been some mis-recording of funds movements, and of course, the Mexico situation is the usual awful third-world one. You cannot make a deal without a slush fund, and these slush funds tend to get out of control."

"I think there is more to it than that..."

"Sure, sure, I'm sure you're right, but our guys are getting right on top of it, and you should just make sure that you forget all about it. Anyway, looks as though you got a promotion out of it. Get a life."

Nick had been made an Assistant Vice President the same day that he had been placed on the Russian Loan team. He thought he deserved the promotion anyway.

But in the back of Nick's mind lurked a ludicrous suspicion. He wondered why a promotion, an appointment to the Russian loan team with a trip to Moscow, and help with finding his lost brother had all flooded in after he disclosed his suspicions about the bank's handling of some funds. But he was desperate to find and meet his lost brother, and he couldn't miss this amazing opportunity.

CHAPTER 9

BETRAYAL

Mother's 'History'. She had apparently kept a wonderfully detailed diary of the events as they happened.

December, 1943 - We were just a small band to be playing in the arena of the great war, but we were a large band to be wandering on the fringes of the battle, looking for our role. There were over a thousand of us left by the time we reached Poland. We were not an army, we were not even a guerrilla band. We were a large village on the move begging to be allowed to fight. There were nearly as many women as men, and some women had their children. The men still had their horses, and the women had articles of furniture and reminders of their homes piled on carts, but no one had much dignity left.

The Cossack homelands had been lost, and we had never really been given a chance to fight. The Wehrmacht had done the fighting on unfamiliar ground, and it had gone badly. The German High Command had never trusted the Cossack Regiments sufficiently to entrust them with the battles they could have won. And so, the Russian Army, after retreating right back east across the northern side of the Black Sea and then north towards Moscow, had reversed the flow, and after the massive defeat at Stalingrad in February 1943, had gradually driven the Germans, and us, west and west again, out and away from our lands. And as the armies retreated, the families had packed their belongings and joined their men in the retreat.

In September 1943, near Poland, we formed a settlement, Kazachi Stan, at Novogrudok. There were Cossacks from the Kuban, Don and Terek. There were also Cossacks who had left Russia after the defeat by the Reds after the Revolution. They had come flooding back, eager to restart the old ways.

The Ataman was a good man called Pavlov. He knew how to organise us into a community. We started to farm again, growing crops and breeding cattle. The old ways were brought back. We wore our old costumes again, danced our old dances, sang our old songs and, of course, told all the old jokes. The Cossack 'nation' was being recreated. The soldiers found the old uniforms they had worn serving the Tsar and put them on with the old decorations. The cherkeska was seen again and, when on parade, the men wore, over their German uniforms, tall fur hats, knee-length boots and flowing capes. The long curved sabres came out along with the ornamental, bejewelled daggers.

We built a community. First, we built a church and then some schools and a hospital. Then we built the community spirit. And for a while it worked. It was the best time of some people's lives, there in the middle of a bitter war.

Because there was always fighting. With a few arms supplied by the Germans and with whatever we captured from the Red Army, we kept the area around Novogrudok free from war. The Russian partisans steered clear of us. And in the middle of it all were Gregor, my father, and Nikolai, my husband. They were the bravest and the best of the fighters, and they went out when the old men were prepared to sit at home and argue about what should be done next. They were men who were respected.

Gregor was now nearing fifty, but still as strong as an ox. His long hair and beard were nearly white, but his eyes were still fierce and angry. He was never about to give up. Nikolai was quieter and softer, but everyone knew that when he was needed, he was as tough and as determined as Gregor.

I did one unusual thing in Kazachi Stan. I learned proper German, and I began to learn English. My brain is tortured with worries, and although I have more than enough work to keep my body busy and tired, I need something to keep my mind from working over and over the predicament we face. For although things feel good and people are happy, I know that it is unreal, and soon we must face the awful fact that Stalin is winning and the Red Army is marching West. The languages fill my mind to stop me thinking. And I am good at them.

The English I am learning from an English prisoner who we held, afraid of his fate if we handed him over to the Germans. His name is Roy Cameron, and he is a doctor. He had an accident and injured a shoulder and both legs. He is almost immobile. But he became very useful to the community, helping with injuries and illnesses, and even helping ladies giving birth. But he needs help, and frequently I am able to provide assistance. He is a gentle man who makes fun of me and my pronunciation, but he is very patient and seems to enjoy teaching as much as I enjoy learning.

Things were going so well that we thought seriously about sending back home for Alexei, who was now nearly five years old and still living with my uncle Piotra and his wife.

"I miss that little Alexei." Gregor said this morning, "He is growing up without me and when I see him again... If I see him... He'll be grown up...." I couldn't tell him that he'll see him again because I don't know whether I'll ever see him again. Nikolai says nothing, but I know that he is always sad.

But the relatively good times couldn't last. First, in June 1944, Ataman Pavlov was killed. Then we were told we had to leave as the Red Army was getting closer and closer. There were other important men with us.

General Pyotr Krasnov was one of them. Krasnov had been our Ataman in the struggle against the Bolsheviks in 1918. He had had a dramatic and varied career. When young, like Churchill, he looked for adventure in a military career and international journalism. He travelled to Ethiopia in the 1890s with a military mission and to Japan in 1904. He was one of the heroes of the Great War, commanding a cavalry corps and receiving the highest award obtainable, the Order of St. George the Victor. When the Tsar abdicated, Krasnov had no hesitation in joining those who fought to re-establish the old ways and the old traditions.

When they were beaten, he left Russia with others and went to France and Germany. He wrote several novels, including the partly autobiographical "From Double Eagle to Red Flag."

Now he was old and in his seventies, and the same game seemed to be about to be played again.

We held an election under the supervision of the German liaison officer, and Domanov became the new Field Ataman. He was one of the 'new generation' who had just emigrated and who had served in the Red Army. A boring man who forgot about the ideals of recreating the Cossack nation.

Boring, but he got us across from Poland through Germany and Austria to Italy, where we were granted land to hold the Cossack nation together, build the new Cossakia, and use it as a base for our military activities. It was near Tolmezzo, a few miles from the Austrian border. This was in September 1944. It was chosen by the Germans because it was one of the few territories they could still command and was out of the path of the advancing Red Army.

Tolmezzo is in the Dolomites, north of Venice, less than a hundred miles from the Austrian border and not too far from Yugoslavia. We were not as happy there, but the camp grew for eight months until by the spring of 1945, it contained 35,000 Cossacks, half soldiers and half refugees.

The Italians resented our presence, and we were constantly harassed by the partisans. Some of the madder young Cossacks were getting out of control. They couldn't see where it could end. Some of the worse elements were committing atrocities as bad as the Nazis. SS members of the Cossack General Staff were initiators, but Cossacks began to be participators.

We couldn't stay where we were, and we couldn't go back.

The Germans were losing the war and the Allies were getting closer. We all felt that this was the solution to our problems. The British, the Americans and the French were not our enemies. We felt we had much in common with them. We felt that they identified with our plight during the Revolution. Their alliance with the Reds was solely to face up to the common enemy, Germany and Hitler. We all felt that at the end of the War, it was the British most of all, with their great traditions of offering a home to refugees from tyranny and oppression, who would be our greatest friends.

April, 1945 – The British are approaching Tolmezzo, and we, although in German uniform, have decided not to fight.

April 27 – The Italians have been coming out into the open, and yesterday the communist band led by the Catholic priest attacked and set our military hospital on fire. It burned to the ground with several wounded Cossacks inside. Today, three Italian officers came to Domanov's headquarters. According to Nikolai, they demanded that we hand over all our arms and *withdraw from Italian soil. The weak Domanov was on the point of agreeing when Nikolai and Gregor said, "We will never put our lives into the hands of these Italians without some guarantees!" But Domanov agreed to evacuate Tolmezzo and leave Italy. So the trek begins again.*

April 29, 1945 – The day was gloomy as we packed up our homes once again. Sheds and huts were demolished. Tents were folded and bundled, wet and soggy, onto the carts. The carts were put together out of crudely hacked planks of wood and roofed with canvas canopies. They held arms, ammunition, wives, babies, children, and everything we needed to raise our families and fight our enemies.

Furniture was stacked high, and pots and pans were piled on top. Horses were fed and then tethered to the carts. We started early, as the sun rose, but the first cart did not pull away until nearly midnight. Near to despair, we headed once more for the Plockenpass, high in the Alps, on the road to Austria.

The mounted units went first, led by Domanov and his staff. We were first in the Don Regiment, then the Kuban, followed by the Terek. Behind wound a seemingly endless column of wagons carrying supplies, personal possessions, and the old, sick, and very young.

Near the head of the column was an old Fiat car carrying old General Peter Krasnov. A rear-guard of several hundred Don and Kuban Cossacks waited south of Tolmezzo to check attacks on the vulnerable procession from the rear by partisans.

The march was appalling. First, we had to fight off attacks by the partisans. Then, the weather worsened as we ascended the mountains to where the narrow road winds precariously round the face of precipitous chasms. First, we were drenched by torrential rain, and then, as we rose even higher, we trudged into the teeth of a prolonged snowstorm. We lost many friends that night, some to partisans bullets, and others to the cold and to falls over the cliff-face.

We left Tolmezzo and passed Imponzo, Cedarchis, Zuglio, Rivo, Paluzza, Casteons, and Timau, through to Passo Monte Croce, which was the Plockenpass at 1,400 metres.

May 3, 1945 – It was late in the evening when we came down into the Gail valley and overwhelmed the small towns of first Mauthen and, further on, Kotschach. We had not celebrated the first of May when we were high up in the mountains. Some of us, late at night, looking out into the snowstorm, wondered faintly whether the Bolsheviks were still surviving back home.

General Krasnov's Fiat had broken down and had to be towed in ignominiously by a transport bus. Our trumpets attempted a brave rousing call as we marched in.

The local German commandant is an elderly man who has not seen much of the war. He stood gazing in amazement as our chaotic band made its way along the main road and filled in every available space in the fields.

May 4, 1945 – Today the British found us. A small advance guard on motorcycles came into Mauthen. The officer carefully dismounted from his vehicle and lit a cigarette. The five soldiers accompanying him held their weapons as he strolled over to us and asked casually, "Who are you?" Nikolai, bearded, with his usual fierce expression, tried to tell him. The English officer nodded, smiled, said, "OK," threw away his cigarette, then climbed back on his bike, and they roared back the way they had come. Perhaps now there will be an end to the war and our uncertainty.

I have fought my way half across Europe to stay with my father and my husband, because each of us believes that the present regime in Russia is wrong. We believe it so strongly that we were prepared to fight on the side of a country that is now thought to be the worst ever in the history of Europe. I have left my beloved son in the care of his uncle and have not seen him for three years. The war looks like ending with the defeat of one evil power but the strengthening of the other. Our only hope now is to align ourselves with the Western Allies and continue the battle against Stalin with new partners. We look forward to working with our new allies. The unknown still waits ahead. The worst has occurred, and Stalin is still in power, but right will one day be done and the three of us will see Alexei again, in freedom.

May 6, 1945 – The local Kreisleiter is Julian Kollnitz. Domanov went to see him dressed in full-dress uniform. We needed someone to take note of us, to do something for us. We looked like such a bedraggled band, and we'd had instructions not to leave Italy.

Kollnitz told Domanov that he had orders from headquarters in Klagenfurt that we were to be let through. He told us that we could continue marching, that the war was nearly over and that there was no more fighting. Domanov confirmed this staggering news by talking on the telephone with Deputy Gauleiter Timmel at Klagenfurt.

Some Cossacks were upset to hear of the end to the fighting, but most of us received the news in fatigued relief. The question now, said my father, was how and who we surrendered to. The overwhelming feeling was that we should surrender to the British. We will avoid the Italians, and we might be alright with the Americans, but we must do everything possible to avoid being anywhere near the Red Army.

Kollnitz told us to move further north. The commander of

the local Volkssturm detachment defending the Plockenpass was Kreisstabsfuhrer Norbert Schluga, who was a native of the Gailtal, the valley of the two villages where we had encamped. He was afraid that we might destroy the area with our wild men and our hungry horses. He told us that the road through the Gailtal was poor and persuaded us to head north into the Drautal, the Drau valley.

It took us three days and two nights to pass through Mauthen on our way to the Drautal. Schluga was very concerned, and stayed on duty throughout our passage with a detachment of Volkssturm to ensure that we took the correct road.

My father was accompanying General Krasnov, and together with Nikolai, we stayed at the Mauthen Hotel Bahnhof, right by the railway station. Domanov brought up the rear-guard and joined us later.

We watched with enormous sadness from the hotel windows as proud Cossacks dragged past on their way north, searching for food for their beloved horses.

German soldiers were going past in increasing numbers, looking even more desolate and desperate than the Cossacks. No love was lost between them, and Nikolai had to rush out more than once to break up fights between Cossacks and those who had once been our allies.

On Easter day, our Cossacks entered the Drau Valley. Crossing the Gailbergsattel, they moved upriver to where the land flattens into a broad plain of fertile grassland. The old and pleasant Tyrolean town of Lienz stands among the meadows, which were large and green enough to provide camping and feeding grounds. We saw shattered people begin to try to create the semblance of homes. The priests held services of thanks.

May 7, 1945 – At 5 p.m. today, we heard that Germany had surrendered unconditionally. Perhaps surprisingly, we celebrated.

Domanov and Krasnov disagreed as to what to do next. Their meeting was long, and they invited my father, Gregor Korshunov, and my husband, Nikolai, to join them. They wanted Gregor, they said, because he was so respected by the Cossacks that they would listen to him when the decision was finally made. Nikolai was the young blood.

Old Man Krasnov seemed to have the strongest argument. "I have been living in Europe for the last twenty years, and I know how they think. I have dealt with the British and the Americans. The Americans know nothing except blueberry pie and the American flag. They are interested in nothing except a glorious American victory. They do not understand the complexities of European history and culture. To them we are the enemy, pure and simple, and the fact that we are Russians means that as well as being enemies, we are traitors to our country. They will have no sympathy for our situation. No understanding of the complexities that lie behind our current position."

"But," responded Domanov, "the Americans are the true believers in freedom of choice for the individual. They are the true opponents of Bolshevism. They will be the country who will face up to Stalin and his plans for world domination. The British are opportunists. They will strike a deal with whoever suits them at that moment."

"I strongly disagree. The British are the ones who showed the greatest support for us, the Whites, during our struggle against the Bolsheviks. I remember when Churchill was Secretary for War during the First War, during the appalling Revolution, he spoke out strongly in our favour. He wanted Britain to come in on our side. He understands our cause. He is our man; we were once his ally, he will come to our aid."

He looked around and saw the astonishment on the group's faces. "You had forgotten that, hadn't you? Churchill, the greatest man this war has produced, is on our side. And not only

Churchill. The Allied Commander-in-Chief in Italy is Field Marshall Alexander. Do you remember," he asked, "that when Churchill was sending men and munitions to help Denikin's armies, Alexander was actually fighting with the Baltic Landeswehr against the Bolsheviks in Courland? On ceremonial occasions, Alexander still wears the Russian Imperial Order bestowed on him by General Yudenitch, just as I have the British Military Cross. You all know that the ordinary Cossacks still believe that the Field Marshall wooed and won a beautiful Russian bride. It is not true, but it symbolises the feeling between our two countries."

He paused and then launched into attack as the younger men hesitated "And the British are not exploiters, as you think. They are the true defenders of moral principles and chivalry. English gentlemen are chivalrous and will fight to their disadvantage to defend those who are in the right. And they know we are in the right," he ended triumphantly.

"But the Americans..."

"The Americans are capitalists first and diplomats last. They will do whatever suits their pockets. We have nothing to offer them but pain."

No one asked Dr. Cameron for his opinion. We all knew what it would be.

It was decided. To surrender to the British and not to the Americans.

May 8, 1945 – A delegation of us headed back over the Plockenpass to find the British and negotiate a surrender. We all thought we were doing the right thing.

CHAPTER 10

RELATIONSHIPS, TRUST?

"It looks to me as though you think you're making off with Joanne, the American princess."

They were changing after their early morning game of squash. The game had been fierce and hard. Jonathan's superior grace and ball sense had been overcome by Nick's greater fitness and determination. Towards the end, as Jonathan realised he was about to lose, he tried a little careful blocking and calling for lets. The third time it happened and Jonathan asked for the point, Nick's temper broke. The racket flew out of his hand and smashed against the wall. Nick stormed off the court, threw the broken racket on the changing room bench, and came storming back with his spare. Jonathan kept very quiet and didn't try any more blocking. Nick went on to recover his temper and win. It wasn't often he lost his temper.

They began to get changed. Nick recalled the comment and challenged, "Does it look as though I think I am making off...? That is not what I think at all."

Jonathan, "You mean you don't think you're making off with...?"

Nick said, "I think the American princess makes off with people and is not ever made off with."

"Ah, well, then. Do you think she is making off with you?"

"I certainly hope not. I am another who does not like being made off with." Nick thought to himself that, in fact, there was nothing he'd like more. "Why are you looking so carefully to see who is making off with whom, anyway?"

"I've known Joanne for some time, and I'm not sure she should be seen with a known Communist subversive."

Nick looked long and hard at Jonathan, who was carefully combing his long dark hair back in the mirror. "Is that your only interest? I didn't think I was treading on any toes. She also says she's known you a long time." Nick felt awkward. "She says she's very fond of you."

"Oh, thanks very much."

"I didn't mean to sound patronising."

"You sound as though you've taken occupation. I hope you realise that she is one of the most desirable properties around. She is not only beautiful, rich, and incredibly well connected, but she is also intelligent, and not only for an American, and she laughs at my jokes."

"But perhaps she's a little left-wing?"

"Yes, she thinks Nixon is a crook, and Vietnam is a capitalist cock-up. And that wouldn't bother you, you Bolshevik. Anyway, she'll grow out of it. You know the saying, the older you get, the righter you get."

"If that's true, then you'll finish up a right fascist in your sixties."

"You mistake a love of the good things in the past for a desire for an autocratic state. The strongest autocracies around right now are the large unions, and if they are going to destroy the good things of Britain, they should be opposed. That's not right or left."

"And they might prevent you from making that fortune that you're about to make by working for an American bank."

Jonathan smiled and raised his squash racket at Nick. "Down," he cried, "you cunning Russian spy. Britain will only survive if infiltrating cads like you are eliminated. Let's have some breakfast round the corner at Renzo's."

The sun was out and shining on the pavement, so they took an outside table. Nick gulped his large orange juice and slapped butter and marmalade on the hot toast.

"Jonathan, can I ask your advice?"

"Give her up, go away, before she breaks your heart. You have nothing to gain but pain, sorrow and distress from continuing this vain pursuit."

"No, seriously for a moment."

"Alright, seriously, but for no more than a moment."

"I have a big problem."

"More than one." Then, seeing the intense look on Nick's face, "OK, I'll shut up and listen for a minute."

"This has to be completely confidential. I shouldn't be talking about it to anyone. So will you promise you will not breathe a word of it to a soul?"

Jonathan nodded, his mouth full of buttered toast. His eyes narrowed, focusing on Nick for the first time. "This does sound serious," he mumbled.

"It is. I've already told you that I found several instances of disappearing funds in some of the accounts I have been working on."

Jonathan looked completely astonished. "You did. But which accounts? What funds? What are you talking about?"

"I can't tell you about the individual cases, but I have found several accounts where funds lent by the bank have disappeared before they were employed by the borrower."

"Several? How many?"

"Two that I'm certain of, others possible."

Jonathan was silent for a while. He poured himself another cup of coffee and then looked into his lap.

"So, what's the problem? We lend to some dishonest people. I know you're involved in a number of overseas loans.

Aren't the borrowing agencies all run by people who want a little cut of what's going, if only to have their own little Swiss bank account?"

"Yes, maybe you're right. But I'm convinced that someone in the bank is involved in some way."

"Well, tell Frank. He'll sort it out."

"I have told Frank."

"And?"

"He tells me he's sorting it out. And I think he has involved Carmina. Who I suspect is CIA. And who says everything will be investigated."

"So, what's the problem?" Jonathan put on a whining American accent.

"That's all they tell me. That it's being sorted out. I never hear what's happening."

"Well, I'm sure he is sorting it out. There's no reason why he should pass on all the dirt he discovers to you."

"Maybe you're right. But say you're not. What should I do then?"

Jonathan thought for a while. "Well, if I'm wrong, it means that Frank is involved in some way, and if that is the case, you will need to go higher up."

"Where higher up?"

"I would suggest that you talk to the Head of the London Branch."

"I can't do that. It could lose me my job if I had no grounds."

"So, what are you going to do?"

"Well, if Frank still has nothing to tell me when I get back from my next trip, I will definitely talk with someone, but I don't know who."

"Perhaps I can help."

"I was hoping you would say that."

"My uncle, as you know, is on the Council of the Bank of England. If there has been some funny business, the Bank of England regulators should have been informed. I could just ask him to have a sniff around and find out whether there has been anything reported, whether a file has been opened."

"Can he do it without letting on where the news came from?"

"My dear boy, Uncle Timothy is the soul of discretion, unlike my old man, his brother, who was the very meat and drink of indiscretion."

"Alright, then, that sounds like a good idea." Nick liked the sound of sharing the burden of his suspicions with a member of the Council of the Bank of England. "But let's wait until after I get back from my trip."

"Fine. Where are you going this time?" Jonathan finished his coffee and prepared to leave.

"This is the big trip to Russia. I leave for Moscow on Monday morning on the 8.30 Aeroflot flight."

"My God. It's on already. I didn't know you'd got this far. What about your brother?"

"He's written back to me. He lives in Rostov. And I should be able to travel down to Rostov to meet him once my work in Moscow is finished."

"You'll probably hate each other."

"That's the risk. He is 36, some seven years older than I am and, as far as I know, has worked in the Rostov docks all his life. But, hopefully, he'll be interested enough in what happened to his mother to give me plenty to talk about. And I have a lot of questions I want to put to him."

"Well, that's going to be incredibly exciting. What a fascinating experience it will be for you. I wish I had a mysterious missing half-brother I could track down as long as he's rich. I think this one of yours sounds a bit too poor to be interesting."

"Typical. Interested only in money."

"Well, my only interesting relatives are the rich ones, and they're all dead."

They got up to go.

"About time we did some work, I suppose. Monday, you said you were leaving?"

"Yes, why?"

"I've got two seats at Covent Garden for Monday night."

"So?"

"Perhaps I'll ask Joanne," he said, walking away briskly and looking innocently up at the sky.

"You bastard!" Nick laughed, but inwardly he wondered.

CHAPTER 11

BETRAYAL 2

Mother's personal History of the end of the War:

May 8 - We set off back to the Plockenpass with trepidation. The delegation was headed by a General Vasiliev, a tall impressive figure whose memories of serving the Emperor in the Cossacks of the Guard were stronger than his negotiating ability. General Krasnov's grandson, Lieutenant Nikolai Krasnov, was there to put the old man's viewpoint, my Nikolai to represent the younger men, and I was there to act as translator.

We fastened a large piece of white sheet to the car as a flag of truce. As we left the village we were stopped by a British armoured car. I explained rather clumsily what we were after, and they told us to head for the Regimental Headquarters at Paluzza.

We climbed over the pass, this time a much easier and quicker trip in somewhat better weather, and headed back into Italy. At Paluzza we were told to go on to Brigade Headquarters in, of all places, Tolmezzo. As we drove in, we were recognised and shouted at by the local peasants, "Cossack barbarians!" Our bad elements had destroyed our reputation there.

We were directed by the British soldiers back to the building that had been Domanov's headquarters last week. There we were received very politely by Major-General Arbuthnot, who commanded the 78th Infantry Division. He invited us into his office and offered us seats. General Vasiliev, a stickler for formalities, insisted on standing, and so we all stood. With a commendable lack of subtlety, Vasiliev came straight to the point. "We have no quarrel with the British. We wish to join you."

Arbuthnot thought he had misunderstood or that my English was not up to the situation. "You wish to surrender?"

"We have never fought against the British. The British have been our allies."

"Allies? You have been fighting with the Germans...."

"We have been fighting against the Bolsheviks. The Bolsheviks are our only enemies. We now wish to join you in fighting the Bolsheviks, just as we did in the past."

Arbuthnot looked slightly amused. "We have no current plans to open a war against Russia. They are our allies against Germany. Perhaps sometime in the future, but I hope not." He looked tired. "Before we discuss anything further about where you are to go and who you will fight, you must, of course, hand over all your arms."

Vasiliev was shaken, although we all knew this must happen at some stage. "Does this mean that we become prisoners of war?"

"No, nothing at all like that. A prisoner of war is a soldier captured in battle. You will be giving yourselves up voluntarily."

I had difficulty understanding this distinction and even greater difficulty conveying it to the others in my translation.

"What is the difference?" asked my Nikolai. "If you surrender, you are taken prisoner. You are a prisoner of war."

"But the war has ended," said the young Krasnov, "so perhaps we cannot then be prisoners of war."

"I don't think it matters what the logic is. They are not calling us prisoners of war, and that is all that matters." Vasiliev was convinced. "We will have a much better status. We will be treated much better." We were joined by Brigadier Musson of the 36th Infantry Brigade, who repeated that we must hand over our arms.

Vasiliev turned to me. "Tell them we cannot decide. We must report back to General Domanov."

The British Generals said they would continue the negotiations the next day in Austria. They then insisted that we have some tea before we set off again for the pass, and although we were anxious to get back to discuss the news with Domanov and Krasnov, we felt we should stay.

Musson insisted on pouring the tea, and the atmosphere was most cordial. Arbuthnot asked young Krasnov whether he missed Russia.

"I left Russia as a baby," explained young Krasnov. "I have lived in Yugoslavia since then. So I miss it, but only as the homeland I have been told about."

"How did you get here?" asked Arbuthnot.

"I fought against the Germans in King Peter's army. I was taken prisoner. I was then asked if I wanted to join an anti-Soviet Cossack unit. My grandfather was with them, and I have been with them ever since."

We chatted politely, and Arbuthnot asked me where I had learned my interesting English. When I told him about Dr. Cameron, he was very interested and asked to meet him. Before we left, General Musson insisted I have a large packet of tea, sugar and chocolate. I was most embarrassed as we had nothing to give in return, but those small gifts had an enormous influence on me and convinced me that, at last, we were in good hands. Arbuthnot was an elderly man who probably had daughters of his own, and he looked kindly at me.

We drove back to the Mauthe Hotel Bahnhof with an escort of British armoured cars. We reported immediately to Generals Domanov and Krasnov and remained discussing the events till the early hours of the morning. The generals especially wanted to hear my version of events, as I was the only one who had understood, first-hand, the statements of the two British Generals.

"They are good men and they can be trusted. I know I am only an ignorant young Cossack girl, but I have met many men during this war, and these two were the first I felt we could trust."

"Including us?" asked the old Krasnov with a twinkle. His humour was returning as, at last, he saw what could be a way out for us.

May 9 - Musson arrived fairly early in the morning, and we reconvened our meeting in the dining room of the hotel. He told me he had met Dr. Cameron, who was now being cared for by the British. We all shook hands carefully, and Musson complimented us on our headquarters. "Rather better than the old place in Tolmezzo."

When we sat, Musson allowed us to dictate where we should take our places around the large central dining table. He made no attempt to take the most prominent position or to place us in an inferior position. "Perhaps I could have a seat near to you? I think I may need to understand what is being said."

"Of course. Over here, over here." Domanov said gruffly, placing Musson at the centre of one side of the table and placing me next to him.

Musson started the discussions with a positive statement about the handing over of our arms. "We think you should keep *your arms until you have settled completely in a decent camp."*

Domanov nodded vigorously at this, and Krasnov kept a clear unblinking gaze on the Englishman.

Musson pulled out a large rolled-up map and asked, "Perhaps you could give us a hand with this map? We are not too familiar with the area."

"Yes, yes," said Domanov eagerly, "we are here. And this is where we are moving to, the Drau Valley."

"Yes, the Drau Valley. That should be a comfortable spot. We think we would like all you chaps upriver between Lienz and Oberdrauberg, and the other chaps, the Caucasians and so on, downstream between Oberdrauberg and Dellach."

"I think he has looked at these maps before," whispered Nikolai to me.

The generals continued discussing precisely where they should pitch their camps. Musson looked greatly relieved and relaxed. He smiled broadly when breakfast was suggested and accepted a large mug of tea. Later, as the conversation warmed, the tea was swapped for wine.

In the afternoon, we were astonished to have two newspaper correspondents arrive at the hotel and ask to interview the "Russian commander".

General Domanov explained, with my assistance, that we were Cossacks and not Russians. "The Bolsheviks made war on us in our own lands."

Domanov pulled out maps to help him explain how we had travelled away from the Don and the Kuban across Europe to finish up in Tolmezzo. "We did not know where we were going or where we would end. We were determined on only one thing, that we should not end up in the hands of the butcher Stalin."

· · • · ·

Later that evening, the first British troops came over into Austria and shepherded the remaining Cossacks into the Drau Valley. I could see that the ordinary British soldiers were amazed by the sight of us. They had never seen anything like us. The Cossacks were in plain German uniform, but they embellished it with tall fur caps, knee-high riding boots, and flowing, although tattered, capes. They were riding their horses with verve and swagger up and down the line creating apparent confusion and clouds of dust. The long line of crudely made carts piled with our worldly goods, men, women, children, baggage, horses, carts, cows, and even camels turned the procession into more of a poor nation on the march than a disbanded army.

May 15, 1945 - The camp is an enormous shambles. There must be 35,000 Cossacks living and milling around. The river Drau, bubbling and foaming, runs through the camp, as does a main road and a railway line. General Domanov has set up his headquarters in Lienz, and so my father and Nikolai spend a lot of their time there. Colonel Alec Malcolm of the Argylls, who is now in charge, has also set up his headquarters in Lienz.

Although technically we are prisoners, it is almost impossible for the British to control us. The camps are not surrounded by barbed wire, and the British don't have sufficient troops to keep a constant check on us. We could leave in small numbers at any time we wanted to. The Caucasians up the river are gradually disappearing. But we Cossacks are keeping together. We look at the tall mountains, and we look around at the strange land and the strange people, but the main reason we stay is because we still believe that we can rebuild the new Cossakia. We know that we can depend on Britain to help us in our opposition to the Bolsheviks. After all, it is only thirty years ago that they helped us the last time they joined us in our fight against the Bolsheviks.

General Krasnov has written to Field-Marshall Alexander to establish exactly what our position is. He reminded him of their common experiences in fighting the Bolsheviks and then went on to describe our current situation and ask him for his advice and assistance. So far he has had no reply.

. . . . .

Yesterday we celebrated Easter in the fields. The bearded Orthodox priests put on their wonderful robes and led the procession into the fields. The whole Drau valley echoed to the chanting and shook as the massed Cossacks roared, "Christ is risen!" We knelt and prayed, we stood and sang, and we hugged and kissed each other. Some of us had built and decorated an altar. It looked beautiful covered with the masses of wild flowers we had gathered in the early morning.

In the evening we lit bonfires and sang and danced around them. Out came the balalaikas and accordions from beneath the luggage, and old soldiers with gnarled hands and hard faces played wild and joyful music. Everyone was wearing flowers in their hair or pinned to their clothes. We danced polkas and mazurkas frantically until we dropped with exhaustion.

May 16, 1945 - Today we met a wonderful man. It turns out that he is Welsh, and his name is Major Davies. He had met and had discussions with Dr. Cameron. He told us to call him Rusty. He has been put in charge of us 30,000 Cossacks, and he has started tackling this impossible task with great humour, walking around introducing himself and giving the children chocolate. He has no chance of controlling all of us, but he works through Domanov, who works through my father, the other generals and Nikolai, who have established fairly firm discipline throughout the camp.

Rusty Davies has persuaded us to change our lavatory arrangements, and this should help to control the sanitary conditions in the camp.

All the British soldiers are very friendly and walk around the camp smiling and observing. They play with the children and give them sweets and chocolates. Any British soldier who walks through the camp is immediately followed by crowds of young children. We feel the warmth of British protection.

A large number of us have been fortunate to occupy an old wooden barracks of the Germans called Peggetz. It stretches for miles, row after row of wooden huts. Some have built crude huts while others are living in tents, some old and some new, provided by the British. We have been lucky enough to occupy a barrack hut. I slept in a bed with a mattress and woke late for the first time since before the war.

We have been allowed to keep our arms, which has surprised and delighted our soldiers and comforted the wives and mothers.

The whole valley is crowded with Cossacks, their horses and their carts. People continuously come and go, asking for names and places, searching for someone they have lost, or searching for a memory they can share. There is an incredible cheerfulness in the camp, with much laughter and dancing covering up the uncertainty and the worry. We are being treated far better than we were ever treated by our own allies, the Germans. We have more and better food, and the British are friendlier and far more helpful. We have only to mention a problem to Major Rusty, than he starts to get something done about it.

I went for a swim today with Nikolai. We went down to the long old wooden bridge over the river Drau and plunged into the icy water, which comes straight off the mountains. There were families taking a swim, the children in the nude playing with a ball, the fathers striding up and down in the shallows trying not to lose their dignity, and the mothers sitting on the river bank doing some washing or mending. We looked at the scene, and I thought of the Don and of Alexei. I didn't look at Nikolai, as I knew I would cry if I did. We swam silently and later lay in the sun on a grassy bank.

May 17, 1945 - The camp is swarming with other nationalities who come and go. I have spoken to Caucasians, Poles, Turks and Jews. I have even heard that there are German Nazis posing as refugees to avoid being captured. It is impossible for the British or for anyone to control the situation.

May 18, 1945 - Today, Major Rusty asked a group of us what we were planning to do. This question surprised us as we thought he would have a better idea than us of what plans were in store for us. He genuinely appears to have no idea of where we are to go. We made it absolutely plain to him that we all wanted to settle in a new land somewhere; some preferred America, some France, some England, but that no one, but no one, wanted to return to Russia. He was surprised, saying it was like him refusing to return to Wales. Vasiliev's wife was there, and she said, "It is no longer home to us. Our home has been occupied by the burglars and the murderers. Stalin is an evil man. He is worse than Hitler. Look what they did to me!" And drew out her hands, which she normally kept hidden, and thrust them in front of Davies, shaking. The nails had been torn out. Davies, although still cheerful, is a puzzled man.

May 20, 1945 - Today, the rumours started flying around. I don't believe any of them as I have seen how kind and under-standing the British are, and I know that they are our friends.

Everyone is talking about 'Forcible Repatriation' and panic sweeps likes waves through the camp. Nikolai is out talking to groups, calming their fears and explaining that no one has anything to gain from sending us back to Russia, even if it could be done.

May 21, 1945 - One of our riding instructors has been giving some of the Englishmen riding lessons. He has tried to show them how to pick up a handkerchief from the ground at full gallop, and how to do cartwheels on the back of a horse. They are not too successful, and there have been many falls and much laughter.

Today the British asked us to round up the many wild horses there are in the area. Taking a great risk, they allowed a group of Cossacks to ride off into the hills in search of the strays. Late in the evening, they returned, each Cossack herding three horses, which they dutifully handed over to the British.

May 24, 1945 - The whole camp is upset by the latest developments. The British have taken away most of our horses. No explanation was given other than that the camp would be easier to administer and hygiene could be improved if the horses were removed to a separate field where they could be cared for all together. A Cossack without a horse is like a soldier without a rifle.

CHAPTER 12

BETRAYAL 3

May 27, 1945 - This morning we were astonished to receive an order from our friend Rusty Davies that we were all to hand in our weapons by midday. We were puzzled by this since we had been allowed to keep our arms, despite Musson's initial concerns, to defend ourselves against Germans and Italian partisans. The British have most of our weapons already because they were stored in dumps. But our officers had their revolvers and their sabres, and we were issued rifles for guard duty.

First, we were told that we would be issued with new standard British weapons. But the handing-in was a tragic sight. Line after line of Cossacks passed by and slung their ancient but valued rifles and pistols onto a growing pile. Some of the men kept their guns and hid them in their huts, under their beds, but most of us were left feeling naked and vulnerable, for we were never handed any new British weapons.

I walked past a huge pile of rifles and other weapons by the side of the road this evening and wondered whether a Cossack without a horse and a gun was still a Cossack.

May 28, 1945 - A positive move at last, although for some reason we are all very uneasy. Major Rusty told us today that a conference has been arranged for all the officers with Field-Marshall Alexander at Spittal, which is only about an hour's drive away. Father is enthusiastic as he feels that, at last, we can begin to talk and discuss about the future, and he has a great admiration for Alexander. I know he worries about Nikolai and me and about the fact that perhaps we shall not see our Alexei again. Nikolai is suspicious, but I told him not to worry, that we had the reassurance of Major 'Rusty'. He had come to Domanov's headquarters that morning, and I had acted as interpreter.

Davies had handed Domanov a written order and explained, through me, what it meant. He said all Cossack officers were to travel the next day to a conference where Alexander would address them and inform them of an important decision taken with regard to our future.

When Davies left, I took the opportunity of talking to him alone. I asked, and was somewhat embarrassed by the implication, whether the conference was genuine and not some form of trick. He assured me that it was exactly what had been said. I asked him why they were moving two thousand Cossacks down the valley when the Field-Marshall could more easily come to talk to them here? He was a little confused and said he did not really know, but that perhaps they had a stage or something similar where they were going where they could all be addressed.

I was still suspicious and said to him straight, "Major Rusty, my father and my husband will be going. Can you assure me that they will come to no harm and will return in the evening?" He assured me that I would see them again unharmed.

Domanov called all the senior officers together at his headquarters and read them the letter. There was complete confusion. Most did not believe or trust the order, but they gradually came round when Rusty Davies' assurance was spelled out to them. Domanov was strangely calm and succeeded in reassuring many. When they finally dispersed to get ready to be on parade at 1 p.m., most were ready to go to find out what it was all about, whereas a few fools were preparing to take off into the fields.

Nikolai approached a lieutenant of the Argylls whom he knew very well and asked him if the conference was genuine. "On the honour of a British officer," he said, "you can tell the women to stop their silly crying."

Domanov is so calm because he is certain that the invitation has come as a direct result of the latest letter written by General Krasnov to Alexander just three days before. They had not told anyone about the letter, but Krasnov had appealed to the memory of their days together fighting with the White Army, and this invitation has come immediately afterwards. Krasnov knows that the Field-Marshall is a gentleman of honour and knows that once he has had an opportunity to explain the Cossack's situation to him face to face, the future will begin to be planned.

The leaving of the officers was a magnificent sight. Because they were to meet the Field-Marshall I wanted Father and Nikolai to look their very best. I brought out our old iron and my needle and thread and set to work on the old ceremonial uniforms. I was so proud of them both when they marched off to the barrack square at Peggetz.

There the cream of the Cossack nation was on parade. They formed up in three columns, one for the Don, one for the Kuban, and one for the Terek. Each had the name embroidered on his shoulder tag, and most wore their old military decorations, many awarded by the Tsar. The ataman headed each column. The square was surrounded by women and children proudly, although fearfully, weeping as they saw their officers go. Nikolai was among them, looking tall and strong. I saw him look back once, but he didn't wave. He wouldn't; that would have been wrong.

Father had gone ahead an hour earlier with Domanov and Krasnov in the staff cars. Outside the gates were a large number of three-ton trucks, fifty or sixty, I should think. At a signal from Major Davies, the three columns marched out of the gates and climbed aboard the trucks in silence and perfect discipline. The first truck started up and roared away, soon followed by the others. They speeded through the camp, leaving clouds of dust billowing among the tents and barrack huts. I waved until the last truck disappeared into the woods.

May 28, 1945 – evening - I wrote the above just after the trucks roared away. It is now ten o'clock, and no one has returned. One thousand four hundred and seventy-five officers have left this camp, and not one has returned. I have been to see General Krasnov's wife, Lydia, and she is in despair. She says that her Pyotr Nikolayevich had never before failed to return when he said he would. I searched for Major Davies and, at first, could not find him anywhere. When I did he was very evasive. Finally, Lydia Krasnov and I found him with the Battalion Chaplain, the Rev. Kenneth Tyson. She asked him, "Are the officers not coming back?" and he replied somewhat nervously, "Well, not here, anyway."

Neither Davies nor the Reverend seemed to know what was happening, but both talked calming rubbish to us and seemed very uneasy.

At eleven o'clock I was asked to act as interpreter again and taken to two officers who had travelled with our officers. I saw two of the trucks standing there empty. My heart sank. I asked where the officers were, and they said they didn't know. I lost my temper then, I'm afraid, and screamed at them, "You lied. You lied! I asked several times, and I was promised that they *were coming back. You deceived us!"*

The officers were embarrassed and said, "We are only soldiers and have to obey the orders of our superiors."

That is the way out for all of them, for the soldiers who obeyed Hitler, for those who obeyed Stalin, and now, of all people, the British, who I trusted most of all.

An abortive meeting was called for all the remaining Cossack non-commissioned officers, but Major Davies did not turn up. I stayed on waiting for news and was woken at two-thirty by Davies with a torch. I set into him, asking where the men were. He was once more vague and evasive and infuriated me even more by appearing to be slightly amused by my fury. When he heard that the officers had dispersed, he said the meeting would be held at eight-thirty in the morning.

I went immediately from this meeting to another meeting in the Lienz hotel, where all the officers' wives were gathered to hear an announcement from Major Davies.

CHAPTER 13

THEY MEET AGAIN

Nick and Joanna met once again in Nick's flat.

Joanna said, "Nick, you look very upset. What's happened? What's wrong?"

"Oh, it's just something I've just read. More of my mother's diaries."

"What is it this time?"

"I can't remember if I had told you. But when my mother died, just before she died, she turned on me and cursed me for a British swine, and cursed the English again and again with a wild rage and a bitterness that I had never seen before."

Joanna couldn't believe this. "How could she? Why? What had you done?"

"I had done nothing. But she screamed at me, **'We trusted you, we liked you and you betrayed us. WHY DID YOU DO IT?! HOW COULD YOU DO IT?!'** She spat at me."

"But I now understand why she was so upset. Can I read you some more from the diary?"

"Yes, if it helps."

Nick tried to explain. "At the end of the war, the Cossacks had to hand themselves into one of the winning nations – to the Russians, or the Americans, or the British."

Joanna said, "Clearly not to the Russians, as they had been fighting them. So to the Americans?"

"They felt the Americans were just seeking glory. They handed themselves to the British, who they respected and admired. They handed over their horses and their guns, and over a thousand officers marched away to meet with the British army."

Joanna said, "That was wise? What was the result?"

Nick continued reading from his mother's diary.

May 29, 1945 - "At 8.30 in the morning, all were assembled outside Davies' office. He did not appear. Then at nine o'clock, a lieutenant turned up and asked me, as interpreter, to read a document to the assembled officers. The document was in Russian, and as I slowly read it out, my voice began to stumble, and I began to cry. It read as follows:

1. *Cossacks! Your officers have betrayed you and led you on a false path. They have been arrested and will not return.*
2. *Now that you are free of their restraining influence, you can speak freely about the lies they have told you and tell us your true wishes and beliefs.*
3. *It has been decided that all Cossacks must return to their homeland.*

The meeting was in an uproar. No one could believe it, and several shouted out that they believed their officers and would follow them wherever they led them. The lieutenant hardly bothered to listen and left as soon as he could, saying that we were now in the charge of Major Davies.

My heart is in agony, my mind in turmoil. I cannot believe that the British, who appeared to me to be our saviours and the one nation who could appreciate our position and give us a chance to keep our nation together, have now apparently deliberately tricked us."

Nick silently sobbed. And Joanna held him tight.

CHAPTER 14

YALTA —
BY THE OLD COSSACK

The old Cossack came back with more tea and poured it out on the little table in the middle of the room.

"You see," he said, "the British knew what Stalin was like. They only joined forces with him because they thought Hitler was a little worse."

"I thought that the truth about Stalin had only come out in Khrushchev's time?"

"Oh no. It was known all along. They just chose to ignore it while the war was going on. In 1931, Churchill made a speech at a meeting condemning conditions in the Russian labour camps. The purpose of the meeting was 'to protest against the brutalities practised in Soviet prison camps and to demand that Russian goods produced by prison labour shall not be allowed to enter this country'."

He was reading from an old copy of *The Times* that he had pulled out from a battered grey filing cabinet.

"Here is some of what he said, 'The conditions there were tantamount to slavery. That government possessed demonic power, and used that power against political opponents, and sent them in scores of thousands to those hideous places of confinement'."

"But wasn't Churchill out of favour and ignored? Wasn't he thought to be a rabble-rousing war monger?"

"Yes, the years in the wilderness. But some people listened, and a large number knew he was right. And yet in the years after he made that speech, the population of the camps increased from 'only' two million to some fifteen to twenty million by the end of the war."

"Fifteen to twenty million?" asked Nick incredulously.

"Yes, the forced labour camps were, and perhaps are, the single most important factor in the Russian economy. And the Allies knew this. They knew it."

"But what happened?"

"Well, you have heard of the Yalta conference?"

"Where Churchill, Stalin and Roosevelt sat in cane chairs in the garden and split up the world?" Nick was handed a photograph of the three unsmiling leaders, Churchill with his cigar, Roosevelt looking very old and Stalin, in military uniform, looking stern and straight at the camera.

"What were they up to?"

"They were up to many things. But among them, all they 'solved' was the problem of the many prisoners of war held by all the different countries."

"But the Cossacks were not political prisoners."

"That's what we thought. That's what we were led to think. But the great powers had other ideas."

"What happened? And why?"

"Well, I've thought long and hard about the why, and I think it was because everyone except Stalin was tired. Churchill had had his great moment. He had won his war, and now he wanted to relax. No, that's wrong. He didn't want to relax. But he was worn. He had used all his great resources to win the war. Roosevelt was a dying man. He wanted to minimise all his problems."

"And Stalin?"

"Stalin was in his element. He was triumphant. He gloried in the position he was in. He saw himself as a conquering hero. He relished it all. Everything he had done before was justified. And he wanted all the traitors back."

"But why did they need to agree?"

"Apart from being tired, they wanted their own back. There were still many American and British prisoners released by the Russians from the Germans who were still in Russian hands. And there were people at home, voters, who wanted them back. No one cared about the hordes of refugees swarming uncontrollably around Europe. The refugees were causing the problem. No one knew what to do with them. It was so obvious, so right, to send everyone home."

"Is that what they did?"

"Let me tell you how it happened. The Yalta Conference began on February 5, 1945."

"February 1945?"

"Yes."

"But that was three months before my mother's Cossacks surrendered in Austria."

"Yes, I know. The policy had been settled well before the surrender."

"What was the policy?"

"A disgrace!" Old Frolov looked angry and upset. He sipped his tea and then carefully wiped his mouth.

"The three 'great' powers," he spat out the word 'great' like a fly he had found in his tea, "had already agreed to exchange prisoners through letters and private discussions. Yalta was chosen as a place where, because the three were together, a formal document detailing the agreement could be signed."

"But why...?" Frolov held up his hand as though stopping a train.

"Wait, wait. All in time. I will tell you the story if you will sit still and listen. I think you are like your mother. She never stopped for anyone."

"The principal concern was for the British and American prisoners of war rescued by the Russians from German camps and still held by the Russians. I will read you a piece from a letter written by Anthony Eden – remember him? – who was Foreign Secretary at the time, to Edward Stettinius, who was the US Under Secretary of State. 'The Soviet forces are over-running the sites of British and United States prisoner-of-war camps very fast, and we know that a number of British prisoners-of-war are in Soviet hands, and no doubt some United States prisoners-of-war also. There were nine camps that held an estimated 50,000 prisoners. Churchill put this to Stalin privately on February 9, and they agreed that the matter should be analysed and settled while they were at Yalta.'"

Frolov pulled out an old pipe and examined it like an old friend. "The Americans had already established what seemed like a sensible policy: to repatriate only 'claimants to Soviet citizenship', but Eden argued forcibly that to follow that policy would be to invite the Russians to dispute the matter interminably. The Americans came round and agreed to include displaced civilians in the agreement as well as prisoners-of-war. Several civil servants then spent long hours into the night arguing about what the prisoners were to be fed, and what work they could and could not be asked to do. The problem of several hundred thousand Russians who did not want to be repatriated was never, never addressed during the entire discussion."

He poured two more cups of tea and put three spoons of sugar in his own cup.

"On February 10, Churchill discussed the matter with Stalin. Eden and Molotov were present. The record of the conversation," he read from another paper, "stated that:

'The Prime Minister spoke of the embarrassment caused by the large number of Russian prisoners in the West. We had about 100,000 of them. He wanted to know the Marshall's wishes about them. Marshall Stalin hoped they could be sent to Russia as quickly as possible... those who had agreed to fight for the Germans could be dealt with on their return to Russia.'

"So, you see, Churchill and Eden knew what would happen to any Russians who had fought with the Germans. And the next day, the day after that give-away remark by Stalin, Eden and Molotov signed an agreement that read as follows:

'All Soviet citizens liberated by Allied armies will, without delay after their liberation, be separated from German prisoners-of-war and shall be maintained from them... These Soviet citizens will be concentrated in definite places to which Soviet repatriation representatives will immediately be admitted... For purposes of internal administration and discipline, these Soviet citizens shall be organised into formations and groups which shall be subject to Soviet laws... The competent British authorities will cooperate with the corresponding Soviet authorities in identifying as such liberated Soviet citizens. They will provide such liberated Soviet citizens with transport until they are handed to Soviet authorities. The competent British authorities will give such assistance as is practicable in providing means of transport for the early conveyance of these Soviet citizens to the Soviet Union.'

There is nothing in this document that actually says that Russians were to be repatriated even if they did not want to go, but this was taken by one and all to be the legal meaning of the Agreement."

"But how on earth," asked Nick slowly, "did the British public accept what was being done?"

"Because, my little Nikolai, your Great British Democratic Public never knew about it. Not only did Churchill and Eden know that the Agreement was disgraceful, but they were so ashamed of it that the whole affair was kept secret. The Agreement was not published as part of the Conference Report, and it was not published and registered with the United Nations. No one was told about it."

Nick shook his head slowly and looked at the picture of the triumphant statesmen.

"You need to remember that Yalta was considered a great success. The Russians had been advancing fast, and the Yalta Agreement seemed to set a limit to their ambitions. Everyone was extremely pleased with the results. No one wanted to reveal an unsavoury side to the Conference."

"I wonder whether Rusty Davies knew anything about all this?"

CHAPTER 15

THE HORROR

Nick found a part of the diary that was fresh, unfaded. It looked as though it had been written sometime later, as though it had proved the hardest to write. For the first time, Polya referred to Nick, as though perhaps she was writing for him.

"And now I must describe the horror. I will try to put down all I remember, but I am not sure that I want anyone to read this. What happened was a disaster, a mistake, not an atrocity. I must try to believe that or I could not now live in England. And you, Nick, if you ever read this, and sometimes I hope that you don't, you must believe that the real atrocities were committed in Russia and that this was an accident, a mistake. A cruel, stupid mistake, but still a mistake. It is not the soldiers who commit the atrocities, but the politicians who create them. Major Davies and his men were good men before the horror, and were good men after. They obeyed orders, and I have heard that expression used many times since then during the Nuremberg trials.

We had been told that in two days' time, May 31st, we

would all be returned to Russia. Fear and panic swept the camp. We were given a strange form of comfort by a request that we should pack up all our officers' belongings so that they could be taken to them. This gave us false hope that they were still alive and could use their possessions.

I went to the trouble and heartache of packing Nikolai's boots, uniforms, belts, underclothes, pipes, and so on, with tears in my eyes and despair in my chest. I could not believe that after all we had been through together, the march across what felt like half the world, I would never see them again. But the stories were that families were split up when sent to the camps. I wrote a letter to Nikolai and one to my father. I did not mention Alexei as I did not know who might read these letters. I found it hard to put anything down because of the possible other readers, but I had not said goodbye when they had left, and so I felt I must say something.

In the end, all I said to Father was: 'I remember the warm evenings on the banks of the Don, when you showed me how to fish, and how cheerful you always were, always smiling, always joking, always kind. That part of you will live forever.'

And to Nikolai I wrote nothing of meaning, as I could not let myself say all that I felt as I would be too sentimental, so I said simply, 'Your son will know you, and he will be just like you. I promise.'

Davies told us that we would travel in comfort. That every effort would be made to keep the families together with all their possessions, to keep the stanitsas together. Special arrangements would be made to accommodate the old and infirm. The crowd looked on uncomprehendingly. Were the British unbelievably naive, or were these blatant lies to ensure that we went along quietly? Whichever, they failed to ensure a peaceful departure.

The camp was immediately put into mourning. Every post

had a black flag, and many families carried crude placards. Mine read, in English: 'Better dead here than return to the SSSR.'

We declared a hunger strike, and a pole was thrust into each pile of food with a black flag.

I saw many sad scenes. I saw men saying goodbye to their horses, which had carried them halfway across Europe. I saw one man take his horse into the woods. I heard a gunshot, and then I saw the man come back with his head held low. I saw an old Cossack giving his cow to an Austrian family.

Major Davies told me to be ready to help him at 7 a.m. on the morning of June 1st. The Don Cossack priest, Vasily Grigoriev, organised a service in the square to start an hour before Davies arrived. We were determined to demonstrate that we were not going of our own accord. We did not want anyone to be able to say afterwards that we had gone willingly.

The Cossack priests arrived dressed in their full vestments and carrying the icons that had come all the way from the Don with us. Before an improvised altar, they began to intone the liturgy. The square rapidly filled up, and soon there were several thousand. I was very near the altar, and I joined in the responses.

Just after seven, Davies' jeep entered the camp. He stopped as he entered the square, and behind him his company formed up. He surveyed the square in despair. He shook his head and backed away, talking to another officer. I had a wild hope that this huge demonstration would persuade Davies that he had no hope of moving this mass of people against their wills. But I underestimated the disciplined obedience and the callous heartlessness of the ordinary British soldier.

A loudspeaker barked out an order that we had a further ten minutes to complete our service. The service continued. Then the loudspeaker barked again and gave us a further five minutes.

We continued singing and praying. I saw Colonel Malcolm arrive red-faced and angry. I saw him waving his finger at Davies and pointing decisively at the line of trucks. A platoon of men advanced on the crowd and were met by solid and stern resistance. All the fitter and younger men were on the outside of the crown, and they linked arms and forcibly held the British soldiers off the crowd behind them. If they grabbed one man, he immediately went down with the others next to him, all holding tight to each other, making it impossible for him to be extricated alone. The soldiers turned away and returned to Davies.

I saw Dr. Cameron come out of the jeep. He limped slowly forwards until he saw me. He waved and gestured that I join him. He insisted that I come with him, as my services as a translator were essential to control the situation. I joined him in the jeep, and we drove away. Did I do the right thing?

The mass of Cossacks was surging around the priests, who continued singing and chanting. Through the crowd, I could see Davies looking very unhappy and uncertain. Then he appeared to pull himself together and ordered his men back."

CHAPTER 16

GOODBYE

Nick's relationship with Joanne had developed considerably. Her mixture of rich, spoilt extravagance and rebellious independence overpowered him. She was used to the best things in life and yet ready to attack them. She enjoyed luxury and yet was continually guilty about her ready access to it. She had read her potted version of Marx and had her relationship with a long-haired radical while at college. Her relationship with her parents teetered on the edge of all-out war. But she never quite did anything to break things down completely.

Nick was finding adjusting to his mother's death hard. He found it difficult to get the image of her white face lying still in the bed out of his mind. Her loss had left him unsettled and vulnerable. He needed stability, and he needed someone he could depend on. But his anger at her past and his burning curiosity about what had happened and where he had come from drove him away from any stable relationships. Joanne's very rebelliousness satisfied his need for an attack on those members of the establishment who might have had a hand in his mother's past unhappy experiences.

Joanne, in her turn, found his mixture of an apparently

steady job and his hidden anger very attractive. She'd had enough of idealistic theorising dope heads and yet was not ready to turn to the grey-suited serious young men who filled the reception rooms of the Embassy. She read the anger in his eyes and it matched her own.

Nick had gone away before, but this time he felt the dinner was a sad one.

Joanne was upset. "I wish I could have come with you."

"You still could. You could book a flight next week and join me when I've finished all the work. We could look around Moscow and then go down to Rostov."

"I don't think travel in Russia is that easy to arrange. And anyway, I don't want to leave my course."

Joanne was doing an antiques appreciation course at Christie's.

"I'm sure you'll fall way behind if you miss a week."

"Well, I'm afraid you will certainly fall behind if you're away for the whole two weeks."

"What do you mean?"

"Well, Jonathan has promised to look after me in your absence. And there are several other young men my mother is keen to introduce me to."

Joanne knew that Nick was unreasonably jealous of Jonathan, and both of them were well aware that her mother thought that she could do considerably better than Nick. She had come to England planning, without much hope, to collect a title for her daughter.

Nick was silent for a while. "Look, I'm going to miss you desperately. Don't make it worse."

"Sorry. I guess I'm just hitting out. Jonathan means nothing more than a very reliable old friend to me. I wish you weren't going."

"I have to go not just because of the job, but because of my brother."

"I know. You have to find out what it was like, what he is

like, what happened."

"I'd like to know what happened to his father, my mother's first husband. I'd like to know what happened to his brother, who stayed behind. And I'm sure that they would like to know what happened to my mother. There will be a lot to talk about."

. . ● . .

Later, as they finished the far too expensive meal, Nick waved groggily for the bill and then put his hand on Joanne's and raised his eyebrows.

She asked softly, "Are you subtly asking what I think you're asking?"

"You go first."

"No, you go first."

"Is this the hour?"

She looked him in the eyes, and he felt reassured.

They sat in the back of the taxi in silence during the entire ride to the house in Holland Park. She sat back against him, and he twined his fingers through hers.

He lit the gas fire in the sitting room and turned the lights down. She appeared to melt into him, and he felt his hands had a precious liquid flowing through them.

The world disappeared, and together they heard a soft, insistent cry. He tasted tears and tried to get even closer, to become one. She wept freely and then clung fiercely, digging nails into his back.

They lay very still, and Nick thought, hoped that they would never move again.

Much later, he remembered her shouting, "Don't go, don't go. I'll never see you again."

PART
TWO

CHAPTER 17

SIMPLE DELIVERY

The flight to Moscow was uneventful. First class was unexpected and full of noisy Russian oligarchs. Nick was tense with anticipation. He could meet his long-lost brother and learn more about his long-lost family.

The hotel was five star and too exotic. He unpacked the Russian clothes he'd been given to wear to make the 'delivery' to a secret destination.

The team meetings negotiating the forthcoming multi-million dollar syndicated Russian loan were long and boring. Nick felt out of place and strangely redundant. He frequently wondered why he was there.

One evening Nick walked through Moscow, exploring. He walked past the Red Square, the Lenin Mausoleum. He went from Myasnitskaya St to Pokrovka, Maoseyka and Kitay-Gorod Mt. He was surprised at how affluent and respectable much of Moscow was. He passed the Et Cetera Drama Theatre, and the Glazunov Academy of Painting and Sculpture. It was snowing as he walked, but he felt that he could cope with a little cold weather. He passed many pedestrians, all well wrapped up in good looking clothes.

Nick had read with surprise that Russia was trying to get Elton John, now the biggest pop star in the world, to perform a concert here in Moscow.

Nick had tried shopping at the Kalinin Prospekt in the most elegant part of the city. He was astonished by the number and variety of shops, theatres, restaurants, and cafes. Maybe Moscow and Russia were not all that out of date and touch? He also remembered reading Pushkin – "Moskva: those syllables can start a tumult in the Russian heart."

He had spent one night at the Moscow Arts Theatre, and enjoyed Chekhov's *The Cherry Orchard*. He felt that the trees should never have been chopped down. Nick would never chop a tree down.

He found the monasteries fascinating – Andronikov Monastery, and Epiphany Monastery, or the few parts of it that had survived, just a block away from the Kremlin. He also saw the 'LANDING OPERATION OF THE TANK SQUADRON' bronze sculpture created in 1975 by Vladimir Dronov displayed in the Muzeon Park, and the World War II memorial 'Great Russia will never turn back; Moscow is behind us', 1975, Panfilov Park, Almaty, Kazakhstan.

He watched the Changing of the Guard at the Lenin Mausoleum. He got to Red Square just before midnight and joined the cluster of sightseers in front of the tomb. The chimes in the Kremlin rang twelve o'clock, and the ramrod-straight guards ceremoniously changed shifts.

It all strangely gave the air of freedom. But was there any freedom? Well, this was 1975, and Leonid Brezhnev was heading a collective leadership that was different from Khrushchev's autocracy. He was guiding the country into higher growth and prosperity. The Gulag system of prison camps was apparently abolished in 1956, and some camps closed down, but...

. . . . .

Eventually, the negotiating meetings reached a break point; they would all adjourn and return to head office in London to consult and re-join in a month's time.

Before setting off to meet his half-brother in Rostov, Nick had to carry out his 'delivery', which he was assured would be simple and easy. Nick was suspicious about the delivery project organised by the CIA. But he was prepared to take the risk in exchange for them finding his long-lost brother. He put on the Russian clothes supplied by Carmina, made sure he had the Russian identity documents also supplied by Carmina, and set off to deliver the 'package' to the suburban flat. He left all his other possessions and papers in his hotel room. The 'package' was a largish envelope, well-sealed, that appeared to contain many sheets of paper. He wondered why it needed a special delivery agent.

The 'flat' was in the basement of a tall building. The front door was in a back alley, fairly dark. Nick knocked on the door. He knocked again. The door opened slowly. A small, nervous-looking man invited him in. The flat was fairly shabby and gloomy. They walked through the opening hallway into a large room containing chairs around the walls and a table in the centre.

Two tough-looking men stared at him as he entered. He tried a friendly hello, "Privet." It was ignored. They told him to sit down at the table. He stared questioningly. And then sat and tried to feel comfortable. One of them sat opposite him. He looked like a bruiser. The other man stood right behind Nick.

"What is your name?" the bruiser asked briskly, looking fierce and unfriendly.

"Nikolai Denisovich."

"Papers?"

"Why do you need my papers? Who are you? I just came to deliver a package."

"We ask the questions. Where is the package?"

Nick reluctantly handed it over.

"And your papers. We need to understand who you are and what you are doing here."

Nick then pulled out his documents and reluctantly handed those over.

He then stood up. "I have now done what I came here to do and handed over the package. I now must go. Please give me back my documents."

The man behind pulled Nick back into his chair and grabbed one arm. The bruiser tore open the package and looked at the contents, raising his eyebrows and let out a long whistle.

"You are not going anywhere. You will come with us."

Nick tried to sound reasonable. "Where do you want me to go? And why, what for?"

Bruiser came round and grabbed Nick's other arm, and they both forced him out of the house and into a waiting car. Nick realised that protesting was useless and just smiled and went along with it.

"You are making a big mistake. I am a simple man, just delivering a parcel I was asked to deliver. You will find yourself in a very embarrassing situation."

The bruiser laughed. And the car set off for the centre of Moscow.

Nick wondered what had gone wrong? Had Carmina and the CIA organised the drop-off wrongly? Was the package much more sensitive than thought, and someone had given the drop away? Had he done something wrong and disclosed something? But he had not mentioned the drop to anyone. And he'd made sure no one saw him leave the hotel in the Russian clothes. Was the whole process just a trap set by Carmina to cover the frauds in the bank? Surely not. Should he stick to his Russian identity or confess to being a naughty Brit? How secure was the Russian identity he had been given?

The car swung into an opening beneath a large imposing ministerial-looking building into an underground car park.

Nick was ushered upstairs, not brutally, but not very kindly, into a small windowless room. The door was slammed shut behind the bruisers as they left him alone to think.

Sometime later they came back and told him he would now be seen by an officer. They guided Nick into a mean looking office, presumably of someone of little seniority. The officer behind the desk didn't stand and didn't look Nick in the eyes, but scanned the papers from the package. Nick looked around the room and noted the small shabby desk and the framed certificates on the walls. There was a window, but little could be seen through the dirty glass.

"Nikolai Denisovich. Is that your name?"

Nick nodded.

"And these are your identity papers?"

Nick wondered what to say, but confirmed his false identity by nodding again.

"And all these other papers? These are your plans?"

Nick tried to be polite. "Not mine. I was asked to deliver them."

The officer then looked him in the eyes with an expression of hatred, scorn and mockery. Nick later learned that this was an expression practiced by all interrogators.

"You expected to make much money with these plans for bringing in many goods through the black market – liquor, food, cigarettes and many other luxuries."

Nick was astonished. "What? I have no idea what you are talking about."

"Of course not. But these papers are just such plans. They prove convincingly that you are involved."

He waved Nick's protests away. "There is no doubt. It will be heard by a court. You can express your protest then."

He slammed his fist down on the desk. "You are under arrest. Take him away to the cellars."

Nick gasped and stuttered, "I must make a telephone call. Immediately."

"NO phone calls allowed. Search him and empty all his pockets. Then take him away to the cellars."

The bruisers dug into all his pockets. All they discovered were the items confirming his new identity. He didn't even have his hotel key. He had made a point of leaving it at reception when he had left.

They then marched him forcefully out and down the stairs – long, long stairs. There must have been a few hundred of them into the dark cellars. They came to a long, narrow, dimly lit corridor with a succession of heavy metal doors bolted and padlocked. They stopped at one door, which they unlocked and opened. Inside was a dark, grim looking cell with grey, damp walls and no windows.

Where was he going? What could he do? He turned to the more responsible-looking bully and asked, "What can I do? I have done nothing wrong. I was just trying to deliver..." the Bully looked a little sympathetic and shrugged. The other bully snorted and pushed him into the cell and slammed the door closed.

Nick looked at the grimy walls and groaned. What was happening? What could he do? His one hope was that the bank would search for him and somehow find him. The hotel would report that he was not there and his bill had not been paid. Carmina would know where he had gone and would try to check whether his 'delivery' had been made. He clung to this hope. Someone would take action.

Even Joanne would start to be concerned if he didn't reappear. Why did she say, "I'll never see you again?"

To his surprise, he was charged in his Russian identity with extortion and black-market crimes, and his protestations of British nationality were completely ignored. He was given no access to the British Embassy. He was not allowed a phone call.

He was interrogated. Nick remembers reading Solzhenitsyn's description: 'interrogation by torture – skulls squeezed within iron rings, prisoners lowered into an acid bath, trussed up naked to be bitten by ants and bedbugs, ... ramrod heated and thrust up anal canal, ... genitals slowly crushed by jack-boot, being beaten to a bloody pulp.'

Nick had thought that the Gulag system had been ended by Khrushchev in 1956 in his criticism of Stalin and his system. But most of the prisons were still here, and the treatment of prisoners did not appear to have improved.

Nick was probably fortunate in only being placed in a bed-bug-infested box the size of a closet. He could not sit or lie down, he could only stand up. He was kept from sleeping for a week and given no water to drink. He was then questioned at night, made to lie face down in a corridor, and fed a few ounces of bread a day.

That stopped him from protesting and claiming to be an innocent Brit. He was convicted at an immediate summary trial and sentenced to life imprisonment.

CHAPTER 18

Not a Simple Delivery

He was sent to a labour camp in Siberia. He travelled in a "Stolypin" carriage – a railway carriage with barred windows for transporting prisoners, called after the Tsarist minister who introduced them. The carriage was full of many different nationalities: Poles, Germans, Ukrainians, Kazaks, Uzbeks, Turcomen, Kirghiz, Russians, Balts, and Finns.

His first cell was a relief. It was lice-laden, bedbug-infested, without windows, without ventilation, without bunks, with a dirty floor, no heating, a day and night light, but ... it was solitary.

Not for long. He was soon in a cell with fourteen others crowded onto seven square yards with a smelly latrine bucket. But at least, at last, he had someone else to talk to. Others who were not his enemies, others who were alive, who were travelling the same experience, with whom he could share the expression 'we', and 'us'.

Some were overtly friendly, and he rapidly learned to mistrust, to be alert to the existence of stool pigeons. He learned when it was his turn to take out the latrine bucket.

He did keep wondering what had gone wrong. Was it all a

plan by Lutz and Carmina to cover up the thefts of the loans? Which would mean that they were involved in the thefts. But how did they get the apparent cooperation of the Russian interrogators? Did that mean that there also was Russian involvement in the thefts? And what had Jonathan and Joanne done to try to help him?

He had protested he was British and, therefore, not involved. But this had made matters worse. He was firstly laughed at and mimicked, and the whole concept of his being British swept aside. One interrogator pointed out that if he really was British, he would not speak such good Russian, and he would be prosecuted as an infiltrating spy who was plotting to damage Russia. He was better off being a Russian criminal.

But would he now ever meet his long-lost brother?

CHAPTER 19

THE CAMP, 1985

Nick started awake with the violence of metal striking metal ringing in his ears. His head shot up, and the rest of his tired body followed slowly and mechanically, shuddering as the freezing air rushed under the thin covers. The ringing outside finally stopped as the camp guard had enough of the cold and left off hammering on the swinging iron pipe.

Nick swung his legs down and quickly, although stiffly, wrapped his spare rags around them before pulling on his black wadded trousers and stuffing them into his valenki – the long felt boots he had treasured since they were first given to him by the old man.

He dropped stiffly down from his bunk and pulled on the worn black wadded jacket that had lain on the bed. The jacket had the same number – S458 – stitched on the back that the trousers had above the knee.

He looked out at the black morning where a thin cold light was beginning to show through the ice on the windows and shivered and tried to shake the numbing ache from his head. But he knew it wouldn't go throughout the day. It was caused by hunger and cold and physical overwork and despair. Then he quickly pulled the thin blankets straight over the sawdust mattress because he saw the Rat come into the barrack room and start to make his way down the aisle between the bunks, banging the metal bedposts with his club, and the old man was still struggling to get ready. Nick hurried over to help him.

When Nick had first met the old man six years ago (1979), the old man had been the tough survivor, a team leader who got the best out of his team, but who used the team to help him get the best out of the camp for himself. Nick was not much use to anyone at that stage. He had been through three camps in four years and had learned little beyond not bothering to protest that he should not be there and not wasting his time telling his story to fellow prisoners who would use his confidence to try to curry favour with the guards. The result was usually a beating and always extra heavy duties, which Nick was decreasingly able to take.

The old man had first seen Nick when he arrived at this camp six years before. It was Nick's fourth camp, and he still had not learned how to keep a low profile. He had been lined up at the front gate with the other new arrivals for the team leaders to pick over and select the best for their team.

No team leader had wanted anything to do with Nick, seeing in him the last vestiges of pride crumbling before an onslaught of unfair treatment. He was in poor shape, beaten physically but keeping going through sheer determination and guts. His public school training was doing him no favours.

He had lost about twenty pounds in weight and looked slightly desperate. His face was gaunt, and he was now missing several teeth. His eyes darted about as he frantically tried to establish and maintain his position in this world. He still thought that superior intellect could overcome all his problems and find a way out. He knew that he was better than the gorillas who ran these places, and he knew that he could overcome them. The beatings were taking their toll, but what was damaging him even more was the isolation of his position. Not just the physical isolation when he was thrown in the lock-up, but the isolation of having no one he could talk to about the situation he was in. In each camp he was an outcast, a loser, and the others all smelled it in him and avoided him. No one cared about the injustices meted out to him when they had heard of many worse, and felt that theirs was worse.

Even in the line-up he was making sacrifices. A small weak looking prisoner, unable to keep standing in the fierce wind and cold, was beaten to the ground by the guard. Nick bent to pick him up and stood in line supporting him, blood running from the little man's head onto Nick's chest. The guard came back and looked long into Nick's eyes. Nick looked bravely back.

"What do we have here? A war hero? Do you think you will get a medal on your chest? Eh?" He stuck his club into Nick's chest every time he said the words, "on your chest, here, on your chest."

Nick dropped the little man and put his arms up to protect his chest. The guard swung the baton one more time into Nick's stomach and sent him flying back, gasping with pain. He lay on the floor vomiting while the other prisoners were selected by the team leaders and marched away.

Nick saw the old man watching him with a faint smile. The old man was tall, with fierce eyebrows, and he was the first to be allowed to choose. He chose no one but waved them away disdainfully and walked away straight-backed and almost arrogant if that could be applied to any camp inmate.

Nick was left with the few dregs and cripples and was taken reluctantly by the weakest of the team leaders, who shook his head and smiled. "So, I am left with this war hero. But he's too young to ever have been in a war. Come on, hero; we'll have to patch you up before we can put you to work."

Nick soon discovered that he was in the worst of the teams of the foresters. They left first thing in the morning, at six o'clock, and had to walk between five and ten kilometres to the place of work through the ice and snow. Many of them were poorly dressed. They started work at seven and finished at five, with no midday meal for most of them. The exceptions were the stakhanovites, named after the famous hero of mining productivity, who were able to beat the productivity norms by twenty-five percent or more. They were privileged to receive a spoonful of soya beans and a hundred grammes of bread. The others sat around the fire and tried not to watch the privilege being consumed.

The razvodchyk, who was the prisoner responsible for calling out the brigades to work, held the morning roll call and ticked the brigades as they left the gate. Outside the gate, their escort, a detachment of the Vohra, the labour camp garrison, waited, mounted in long grey coats and fur caps, and with bayonets.

After the first day's work, Nick realised he would not survive this camp unless he did something dramatic. The work was hard, harder than anything he had experienced so far, but the conditions were unbearable. His brigade worked most of the day waist-deep in snow in clothes that were not good enough for a walk in the park on a winter's day in London.

The only relief was the short sit round the fire at midday when Nick was able to talk to some of his brigade. He discovered from Polenko, a thin, stumbling man who was eager to advise Nick in the apparent hope that Nick might, in turn, help him keep his position, that they were a dispirited lot who did not expect to last much longer. He was told about the competitive system that ensured a drive for productivity. Each brigade was divided into teams of four or five, and each team's output was measured against a norm in terms of numbers of logs. Each team divided its work: one cut the pines down, another cleared the trunks of branches and bark, and the other two cut the trunks into logs of a certain length and piled them at the side of the track in stacks two metres high.

A foreman toured around the teams, counted their piles

and stamped them. These counts then formed the basis of measuring the team's performance against norm. The norm was almost unobtainable even to experienced Finnish foresters, of whom there were a few. Stacking a hollow pile was the skill most appreciated. Those teams who, sometimes by bribing the foreman, were able to outperform the norm by more than twenty-five percent were classified "stakhanovites" and took their food from the "third cauldron" at night. This meant that as well as the single spoonful of boiled barley, they were given a small piece of fish, usually boiled herring. Nick's team was clearly not among the stakhanovites, and Polenko was a liability even to them.

Nick was lucky to receive the single spoonful and the half ration of bread in the evening. Because of this threat, the teams were ruthless with members who could not perform and ensured that they were rapidly replaced, and equally, hard workers were attracted to the best-performing teams so that all could benefit from the higher output. No one lasted longer than two years working in the forester brigades, and most left for the hospital or straight to the morgue.

As the time to return to camp came closer, the zeks' spirits rose, and one or two of them actually sang. They handed in their tools and sat around the fire, waiting their turn to be called to march back. Hands were raised to the fire, hands that were blistered, raw, frostbitten, dirty, blackened, and bleeding. The end of the day dragged them down; their faces were exhausted, drained, and yet they faced their five-mile walk back to the camp. Nick had seen several collapse already, and when the call came, he felt that he could hardly move, felt that he'd like to stay there by the fire all night.

But the walk back went better than the walk out. There was a swing in the step as they thought of the scanty shelter and the meagre rations waiting for them. Nick was supporting Polenko as they neared the camp, although he could have done with some support himself. He saw the black lines of shambling humanity converging on the sanctuary of the lit gates of the camp.

Polenko was not a nice man; he had apparently survived his time by ingratiating himself with the nearest soft touch. Nick regretted helping him several times on the trip back, but felt he couldn't abandon him to almost certain death. When they arrived at the guard house, they were taken individually and brusquely searched. Polenko scuttled ahead of Nick and was quickly through the gate. The guard soon found a small piece of bread in the side pocket of Nick's jacket and produced it triumphantly.

"Out! Outside! All of you. Total search!"

The members of the brigade still outside groaned and cursed Nick. They were taken to one side and there, in the snow, forced to strip almost naked. Only when the guards were satisfied that they had nothing else concealed were they allowed into the camp.

They then went to their barracks for their mess cans and queued outside the kitchen. They were not only tired but very cold and now late for food and destined to get the watery scraps left at the end of the evening. Nick was not popular, and every zek who passed him cursed him silently. One shouted to the brigade leader, "Teach that new boy to think before he steals. Get him off our brigade!"

Polenko was not to be seen. No doubt he had finished his scraps and hidden them from Nick. Nick wondered how he had managed to steal the bread from the stakhanovites.

As Nick left the kitchen and gobbled up his gruel standing in the snow, he saw the tall old man with the beetling brows standing in a doorway watching him. Nick turned away, strangely embarrassed to be seen to be so ravenous and incautious. A wise prisoner saved part of his bread for the next morning, but Nick couldn't contain his hunger.

CHAPTER 20

LEADERSHIP – CAMP 4

The next day Nick had been relegated to an even less competent team and saw his slender hopes for survival slip further away. He spent the day in a futile attempt to organise the team into a more productive use of their efforts, but had his attempts spurned by the team leader, who read into his efforts an attempt to usurp his position.

He returned to the camp weaker and even more dispirited. Polenko, now on a different team and still very much alive, made himself scarce. Nick missed even his untrustworthy friendship.

That night in the barracks, he looked enviously at a group of urkas laughing and plotting around the stove in the middle of the room. Urkas were the long-term criminal prisoners who Nick had realised controlled much of life in the camps. They were hard men who were used to fighting and scheming for themselves, and they were resigned and adjusted to a life in the camps. They had no vague hope of a life on the outside and wasted no time pondering the unjustness of their fate. They got on with living in the environment they found themselves in and set about conquering it. As a result, they controlled the portion of camp life left to them by the camp guards.

They despised the "byelorutchki", the political prisoners who spent their time bewailing their lot and blaming the political structure, or even, on occasion, forgiving the government but blaming the bureaucracy for having made this terrible mistake. They despised the intellectuals who were there for their words or even their thoughts, but who could not think their way out of their current position.

Nick listened to them plotting a way of obtaining more of the food from the kitchens to use for bribing the guards to obtain better work allocation.

"The best jobs are always taken by Kilgas," he heard them say on several occasions.

Kilgas was a man they obviously respected, feared and hated in equal measures.

"The Cossack should be taken care of," one man shouted.

"He'll be taking care of you if you don't keep your mouth shut."

"What with his Cossack sabre?"

"He's no Cossack. Real Cossacks can't organise work like this one. It's all they can do to pull up a turnip before it's rotten."

"I think," spoke up a squat, hairy man with flat, meaty hands, "we forget about Kilgas and let him get on with it. We have to try to be as clever as he is, not try to get rid of him. What he does should be possible for us. He opens the way for us."

The name rang a bell for Nick, and he tried to remember where in his mother's papers he had read it. He was, for the first time in a long time, excited with anticipation. Just as the teams grew excited at the thought of returning to the very camp they hated, he was growing excited at the unreasonable expectation of meeting someone who was a Cossack and who might have known something about his mother and what happened in the war.

Few people spoke to Nick, and so he found it hard to ask questions about a man he didn't know. The next day he had a plan for improving his lot. He made sure he marched out to the worksite next to his team leader.

"I have an idea that might help us reach our norm. I want to give it to you so that it can be yours." Nick spoke so that only the team leader could hear.

The team leader, a Pole called Gerling, snorted with derision. He was a philosopher who was in the forest only because his spare time activity of gymnastics had made him fit and muscular, but he despaired of ever raising the output of the team to anywhere near the norm.

"Can I tell you about it?" Nick took the second snort to be a yes and so proceeded with his ideas.

"I noticed yesterday that you were choosing to take down the smallest trees."

Gerling snorted.

All the weaker teams chose the smaller trees and left the larger ones to the stakhanovites.

"Is it because we are afraid of the stakhanovites? Do they have first option on the larger trees?"

Gerling turned and looked at Nick for the first time, with derision all over his face. "There are plenty of large trees for everyone. But can you see this lot," he jerked his head backwards, "cutting up and carrying a large tree?

"Ah, I see," said Nick, who had suspected this. "What if there were a way..."

"A way? What way? You're crazy as well as stupid. Don't try any of your stupid tricks with us."

"Let me tell you about it. If you don't like it, you don't have to use it, do you?"

Snort.

By the time they reached the work site, Gerling, still sceptical, was ready to try Nick's ideas. They headed for the largest tree, one more than twice the size of those they had brought down the previous day. The team protested feebly.

First, they took down a small tree alongside the large

one. And in doing this, Nick introduced his first innovation. The trees were all being cut down by one man using a long, thin, curving saw. There was a skill, a knack, about using this saw that was not easily mastered. If worked too fast, it bent and buckled, but if worked too slow, it jammed in the wood and had to be wrenched free. Nick's innovation was to take a branch and bind it to the other end of the saw. With no twine available, he had to sacrifice one of his vests which he tore and twisted to use as a binding. Then with one man at either end the saw was kept taut, and the tree was down in half the time.

The team was exultant, and Nick saw a gleam of hope in their faces for the first time. Gerling, whose idea, of course, it was, was proud as punch.

Then they tackled the larger tree. They gave up when they realised that the trunk was too wide to allow them to use the full length of their two-handled saw. So they chose the one next door that was just a little narrower. As Gerling and one man made impressive progress through the fat trunk, Nick saw the small tree cleared of branches and smoothed of any projections and then cut, against the team's strong protests, into lengths too small to qualify for the team's norm. He placed these shorter lengths carefully in the path of the descending tree. The snow was thin on the ground and the ground sloped, although not excessively.

Nick rushed back to the tree where Gerling was sweating away triumphantly. They carefully placed the last cut to ensure that the giant came crashing down right on the carefully laid path of logs. Then they threw themselves furiously on the monster and stripped it of all its branches. As the last few came away, the huge trunk settled firmly on the smaller logs placed underneath it.

"Now. Let's roll her down to the road."

With a roar, they surrounded the giant log and heaved. Soon she rolled gradually forward, and Nick had the smallest man pick up the rollers as they came free behind and rush them to the front to take the load there. The log never got out of control, which Nick blessed later as he lay in bed going over his triumph, and they arrived at the roadside with an enormous cheer. In no time they had reduced the log to the required lengths and were up again carrying their rollers to select another large tree.

That evening, the foreman was amazed to find that Gerling's team had beaten the norm by ten percent.

The next day they beat it by thirty percent, and that without too much cheating in building the pile.

The next week they celebrated with a piece of fish with their gruel and with seven hundred grammes of bread instead of four hundred. Gerling was the hero of the brigade, but most zeks knew or suspected Nick's role.

Then Nick felt that he could ask who Kilgas was. Gerling spat, "Don't have anything to do with that man. He is trouble to everyone except himself."

But he pointed him out at the next mealtime, and it was the old man with the fierce brows who had turned him down on his arrival.

The old man was tall, taller than most of the other zeks, and his skin was smoother and almost looked tanned, as though he had spent the last few summers at Cannes and his winters at St. Moritz rather than the whole year in the depths of Siberia. He held himself high, too, and used his piercing eyes under beetling brows to dominate whoever he came across. His strong personality intimidated even some of the guards, but he used it with caution. He held back some of the power when handling the most difficult of the guards. He could efface himself when necessary to avoid humiliating guards who were sensitive to their position and the respect they thought they deserved.

Most of his hair had gone, but the dome of his head shone with vigour. Most of his teeth had gone with his hair, but he still spoke clearly through a long straggly moustache.

His voice was deep and powerful, and he delivered himself well, with clear, complete sentences and compelling logic. The accent was strange and guttural, but then most of the zeks had strange accents. Ukrainians mixed with Armenians, with Kazaks and Uzbeks and Turcomen and Kirghiz, and Russians were not in the majority.

He mixed with the intellectuals in the camp to the extent that there was any mixing, but he was also able to mix it with the gangs and their leaders, outfacing them whenever there was a power struggle without letting matters break down into a war.

He was respected by most, but not liked. He did no favours without expecting equivalent favours in return. He was feared by many and hated by a few.

His name was Kilgas. When Nick had first heard it shouted, he had started. But it was probably a common enough name, and he soon forgot to wonder whether it was the same Kilgas.

CHAPTER 21

THEY MEET

Nick watched Kilgas whenever he saw him and followed him into the mess hall when he could. He was searching for a way of approaching someone who was clearly not very approachable.

One evening he slipped into the queue a few places ahead of Kilgas, thinking he could find some pretence for speaking to him when he saw Polenko just ahead of the good and gullible Gerling. He saw Polenko trip Gerling as the hungry man turned from the cauldron, and Gerling's mess can go down. Before it hit the floor, Polenko had caught the fish and the potato, put them in his own can and turned for the door. No one appeared to have seen what had happened except Nick. His temper, never well controlled before but in good check for the past few years, flared.

"You rotten bastard," he screamed, reverting as most do in times of crisis, to his native tongue, "come back here, you dirty cheating shit!"

He shot across the room and grabbed Polenko before he left the hall. "You bastard! You'd take the final meal from a dying man!" He went berserk and would have killed the Pole when he felt himself pinned from behind. As he struggled, a soft voice said in his ear, in near immaculate English, "Calm down, calm down, this won't do anyone any good."

The shock of hearing English for the first time in many years stopped his anger, and he watched immobile as Polenko left his mess can on the floor – with two potatoes and the fish on the floor – and backed away through the door with both hands up, palms facing Nick. Gerling had picked himself up and came over to reclaim his food. "Thank you, Nikolai. You can have his potato."

Nick grabbed the potato and threw it after the retreating Polenko. A scuffle of hungry men engulfed the Pole and his potato.

The guards finally moved towards the disturbance, and so everyone rapidly dispersed. Nick found himself back in the queue, still shaking with anger.

When he had finished eating, he found the old man walking next to him. He looked closely at Nick and finally said, in pretty good English, "Well, my dear young chap, that wasn't very polite, was it? Where did you learn that sort of language?"

Nick was astonished but he kept silent. He had stopped claiming to be a wrongly accused Englishman since it had done him nothing but harm. He had been tricked a few times into telling his story to an apparent friend, only to regret it for days later. So now he kept quiet.

"Come on, no point in denying it. I heard the swearing, and if that wasn't the King's English, I'm a Dutchman."

It was good English, but it was English learned by a foreigner, and learned some time ago.

"No one here thinks you're Russian, but then no one cares."

"What is it to you?" asked Nick in Russian.

"I enjoy talking in English. I haven't done it for some time now – some thirty-odd years..."

"Where did you learn it?" Nick asked, relapsing with relief into English.

"That's better. You'll find you enjoy it. No matter where I learned it, but I enjoy speaking it, although it isn't wise to do so constantly in front of others. They resent it. I hear you are quite an organiser, is that right?"

"Well...Gerling..."

"Come, come, no mock modesty here, my friend. I have just lost one of my young men. I like a well-organised team."

"Are you inviting me to join your team?"

"You English! I thought you were the masters of the understated. I didn't want to be so forward as to actually issue a formal invitation." The mocking tone and the twinkle in the eyes could have been those of an English don.

"I don't feel I can leave Gerling and his team...."

"Oh! Team loyalty and all that. Splendid sentiments. But you'll find they will abandon you as soon as it suits them. And you have already done them an enormous favour. You've saved their lives. I won't appeal to your sense of self-interest by telling you that my team is the best organised and gets all the best jobs, because your interest is in sacrifice, not survival, but I will tell you that you will have a lot more fun and some interesting conversations with me. Finally, of course, you could think about me. I am desperate for interesting conversation, starving for company."

His personality was overwhelming, so Nick gave in and joined his team. Gerling shrugged his shoulders. The old man gave Nick lessons in camp survival.

"The secret, Nikolai Denisovich, is to concentrate on the day ahead and forget about the next day or the year ahead. You must survive today before you lay out your grand plans for the next year or for your escape. If you survive three hundred and sixty-five days, you will find that you have got through a year."

Nick nodded, glad to hear someone speak to him in anything other than a shout or a grunt.

"Next, you must forget all about helping others except specifically in order to obtain a returned favour. Helping that little

Jew in the line-up was stupid. The man will be dead within a few weeks and will never be able to return the favour."

His manner of speech was methodical and systematic, totally unlike the almost incoherent ramblings that Nick had met so far.

"So, why are you giving me this advice?"

"Aha! Don't ask. Just be grateful someone wants to look after you," he snapped and went on in a hurry. "Forget all about your principles and pride. Forget everything you learned about self-sacrifice, about holding your head up high. Here it will get you nowhere. Here you want to keep a very low profile. Don't stand up for yourself or anyone else."

"But you..."

"Some of us can get away with it. But not forever."

His Russian was a mixture of many accents. The grammar was accurate, the vocabulary was extensive, but the source confused.

"You are Kilgas?"

"Yes. Alexander Kilgas."

They were lining up for their food as they talked. Ahead were short dour characters, wadded against the cold, stamping their feet, muttering short phrases of protest, of complaint. Behind them were more of the same.

The old man stood out against most of them.

CHAPTER 22

CAMP TEAMWORK

They were out on the worksite when the old man started to probe Nick about his identity. The wind screamed around the half-built power station, and the thin snow piled in dirty drifts and penetrated every corner. The old man's team had one of the easier tasks, deep in the heart of the giant structure. The old man had done some dealing to get the team into this position and had provided the guards with many cuts of fat. Subsequently, he had done some fighting to keep the position. The team could thank him for their lucky situation. Other teams working on the outside of the building were falling in the freezing conditions. Harsh, barren concrete laced with rusting iron reinforcing bars seemed to fit well in the barren, frozen landscape. Rather better than on the South Bank of the Thames, thought Nick when he first saw the enormous hulk as they trudged their way towards it from the camp.

The team's job consisted of building indoor partition walls. The deliveries of building blocks were erratic, so they had periods of enforced idleness followed by periods of frantic work as they struggled to complete their quota. Although the work was backbreaking, the team found it strangely satisfying and were never happier than when they were working in unison, two men unloading the truck into a neat pile, two others picking five at a time and carrying them up the ramp to another neat pile in the centre of the room. Four of them were working their way across the open space of the room, two laying blocks low and two laying them high, on ladders, which they moved as they completed a segment. The boys building the lower part of the wall speeded up to keep ahead of those above, who in turn raced to try to catch up with the ones below. The babble was continuous as each man shouted to the one next to him in the chain to hurry and keep up.

The old man had organised this incredibly fast production line together with Nick. He strode around the group, shouting encouragement, hitting slow workers, jumping in to give a hand when a pile of blocks collapsed, and cleaning the joins of surplus mortar to provide a neat finish.

Nick was responsible, along with a huge Ukrainian called Mikhail, for distributing the blocks to those building the wall. He carried blocks to the ones working below, piling them up just ahead of their progress. For the ones working on the ladders, he had to have piles waiting so that as they needed blocks, he could throw them up to them. The large Ukrainian could carry twice as many blocks as Nick, but was a clumsy thrower. The men laying the blocks yelled incessantly at Nick and the Ukrainian, berating them for their tardiness and cursing them for delaying the work. The angriest was the fastest layer, a lean Armenian with wild hair, who caught each block in one hand while slopping on the mortar with the other. He always seemed to be one block ahead of Nick and never stopped screaming at him. Trying to be too clever, he started to snatch the blocks out of the air as Nick tossed them up to him. Then he missed one, stubbing his thumb on it as he snatched. The block fell towards the layer working below and Nick, in his stupid self-sacrificing way, threw himself to catch the block, saved the zek from having his head crushed but landed with a thud on the concrete and grazed his side.

The Armenian let rip a string of curses, shaking his hand in pain and accusing Nick's mother of having done several unmentionables before giving birth to such a foul unnecessary thing as himself. Nick rose, bleeding, and flew at the ladder, bellowing all the curses that erupted out of his past. The words were English and did not sound half as effective as the Armenian's curses, but they released some pent-up anger and frustration for Nick. Although no one understood the words, the meaning was clear, and the zek who had been saved and the Ukrainian grabbed Nick and held him away from the ladder and the Armenian.

The old man roared, and a few minutes later all was forgotten, and the work was again in full swing.

The mortar was sent ready-mixed by another team and dumped off the back of a truck beside the blocks. The timing and quality of these deliveries were another constant source of bitter complaint. The mortar was always too watery or too dry, the mixture was wrong, or it had not been mixed at all. Other members of the team were scooping it up in buckets and carrying them, two at a time, up to the layers. The mortar would freeze if left too long, another reason for the frantic dash to complete the wall. But the main reason was the old man's determination that if the team were to be asked to do anything, they would do it better than anyone else. Through power of personality, he had welded this disparate, desperate bunch of broken men into a well-oiled machine. And they enjoyed it; they finished the day exhausted but satisfied. And they were not completely exhausted because they were able to take breaks as they waited for the next delivery of blocks and mortar.

When Nick had first joined the group, he was amazed by the organisation and productivity, and thought it must apply to the entire workforce at the power station. But others who had worked on other teams explained that their team was unique.

Elsewhere, the main aim was to avoid work and minimise the strain. Team leaders were admired for finding somewhere to hide, some way of avoiding the job ahead, and some acceptable excuse for not meeting the norm. Shirkers were not welcome on the old man's team. If anyone tried to duck a job or slow the process down, he was soon out of the team.

By the second year, Nick had learned the work and was seen by most to be the old man's right-hand man. Nick was seen to be a thinker who could also do his share of the work. He had struggled at first but gradually came to grips with the cold and the hard labour. He also had a team leader who appreciated his ability to think through a situation and who relied on him for advice when setting out the division of tasks and the organisation of the work. It was Nick who had thought of having two layers working high and two working low, thus enabling four to lay instead of only two. As it was the most popular and prestigious job, it created a competitive race between the upper and lower workers.

They were taking one of their forced breaks as they waited for another delivery. The team was huddled around a fire made up of ends of planks and other scraps of timber and boarding. The old man had found a corner where they were less exposed to the wind and signalled Nick to sit next to him.

CHAPTER 23

THE OLD MAN DIGS

They sat like this frequently in the odd moments they snatched away from the constant struggle for survival. The old man would teach Nick how to survive and talk about literature, art and history. He obviously relished intelligent conversation and liked playing the part of the teacher to the poor, innocent Nick. He avoided at all times talking about himself or his past, and had never asked Nick about his.

He delighted in exposing Nick's naivete.

"What was all that about? You still playing the hero? Learned nothing yet?"

"If we're to work as a team, we need to feel we care for each other."

"And so we do, so we do. But there is a limit to sacrifice. And you go over that limit. Certainly, we want the team to feel that we all have a common aim and that we are working together to achieve that aim, but at the end of the day it is fear that drives them on and not just fear of starvation or solitary confinement, but fear of us, fear of our disapproval, fear that they will no longer be part of the team. You, with your sacrifices, and your willingness to mix in with them, even though they are most uncomfortable in your presence, reduces the division and so reduces that fear, and therefore takes away a further motivating force enabling us to achieve our best performance."

Nick laughed.

"What's so amusing?"

"I never thought I'd be discussing the relevance of different management techniques in the middle of a Soviet labour camp. One thing about management here is that it ought to be simple and straightforward."

"But that is where you and the entire camp organisation are so wildly wrong. That is precisely why the output of the Soviet Union since the War has performed so badly compared with the West. Or so you have told me."

"Aren't you worried about helping the Soviet economy?"

"No. I have no other. Anyway, Nikolai, I am tired of talking about these generalities. I now want to know who you are, where you are from, and what you are doing here."

"And can I know about you?"

"Perhaps, but let's start with you."

Nick never knew why Kilgas had chosen this moment to start exploring the past. Perhaps he sensed that he was now growing old, and it was a last attempt to reach out to that outside world that he would otherwise never know.

"Well, I'm English, as you so rapidly guessed, and everyone else has chosen to ignore."

"But how did you get into this infernal place?"

"I don't know. I don't know what happened. I don't know why I am here. I think it may be something to do with spying. But no one has accused me of that."

"Tell me exactly what happened to you."

"I was visiting Russia as a businessman. I work for an American bank."

"That's innocent enough."

"But I had been asked by the CIA..."

"The CIA?"

"The Central Intelligence Agency, that's the American spying department. They asked me to do a simple delivery of a package to an address in a suburb of Moscow."

"And what happened?"

"They gave me a false Russian identity with papers and clothes. I took the subway, the underground, out to the suburb. I walked to the block of flats, and when I went in, they were waiting for me."

"The KGB?"

"I don't know who they were. They didn't take time to explain."

"So then they accused you of spying."

"No. That's the odd thing. They accused me in my Russian name Nikolai Denisovich Kamenev."

"And what is your real name?"

"Nicholas Cameron. And they accused me, not of spying, but of black-market operations."

"Black-market operations?"

"And later treason. And other matters."

"It all sounds a little vague."

"It was certainly confusing."

"And you didn't show them your passport."

"Because that was back in my hotel room."

The old man looked puzzled for the first time. Nick recalled that the old man had been in the camp for more than thirty years, and any outside activities must seem a little puzzling to him.

"But didn't you tell them that you were British, that you worked for an American bank? Being a spy must be preferable to being in here for life for treason."

"To start with, I kept up the pretence, thinking that perhaps there had been some mistake and that I would be let off when they discovered the mistake.

"But when I realised that there was no mistake and that

a trial, if you can call it a trial, was getting closer, then I told them who I was."

"And what happened?"

"They didn't believe me. They took no notice. Not even when I ranted and raved. I never found anyone who spoke, or would speak, English."

"They didn't want to know."

"You can say that again."

"They didn't want to know."

Going back over it all was a great relief to him. For the first time, he was able to get rid of the burden, to share the puzzle with someone else. He had all but given up hope of reaching a solution and had fortunately had to divert his energies to the question of survival. But now all the bitterness came back. The anger at the wasted years, the unfairness of it all.

"I should think you were a little upset."

The mimicked English understatement for once was not amusing.

"Upset? Upset? I was absolutely flaming furious!" Nick was standing, shouting, waving his fists, almost in tears.

"Calm down. I understand. Let me try to help you. We'll talk it all through. Why did this CIA ask you to deliver this parcel?"

All the questions that Nick had asked himself a million times came out. He was glad to try to answer them.

"I don't know. I think because I spoke fluent Russian."

"Why do you speak fluent Russian?"

"My mother was a Russian emigre. We spoke Russian all through my childhood, and I studied it at University."

He wondered whether to explore the Cossack background, but decided to leave it for another time.

"I'd like to talk about that later. But now tell me, don't the CIA have many agents who could have done this delivery?"

Nick had wondered about that.

"Well, they had done me a favour, and so I suppose I felt that I owed them one in return."

"What favour had they done you?"

Nick hesitated. "They found my brother for me?"

"Your brother?"

"Yes. Well, my half-brother. My mother left a son in Russia before the war, and I was trying to contact him."

"Thirty years later?"

"Well, I didn't know about him until then. My mother died, and only then did I find out that he had existed at all."

"And the CIA helped you find him?"

"Yes. They tracked him down and gave me his address."

"And you were going to visit him?"

"Not when I was picked up. That was going to be later, after I had made the delivery and finished my business in Moscow."

"What was your business in Moscow?"

"My bank was negotiating the lead position in a large syndicated loan for Hungary."

The old man was silent.

"International banks now make large loans to countries. They syndicate the loans, they share them between several banks and so spread the risk."

"I don't know what you're talking about. It seems like a fantasy world. American banks' lending money to Hungary."

"Well, it happens every day. In fact, the banks are desperate for the business. Or were." He remembered that he had been out of touch for ten years now. "The property market crashed, the share markets crashed, and then the Middle Eastern countries trebled the price of oil, and they were soon swimming in dollars as they were all paid in dollars. All the under-developed countries were desperate for finance to build factories to try to catch up with the rest of the world, and so the dollars deposited by Saudi Arabia, Kuwait and Iran were recycled to the lesser developed countries in the form of syndicated loans."

The old man's mouth dropped open.

"Good Gott! Perhaps I have been better off hidden away in here. The world sounds like a very different place. I'm not sure

I could cope with it."

"You'd be a winner anywhere."

"You call this being a winner?"

"Anyway, I was over here helping with the negotiations on the Hungary loan. It was a new job for me. I hadn't done much in syndicated loans before, and the bank had never chosen to use my Russian until now."

"Did the bank know about your little job for the CIA?"

"No. Or at least I think not." Nick thought back to the first time he'd met Carmina, the CIA man, and they had been introduced by Lutz at the American Embassy.

"But the big question must be, why has no one made a fuss about your disappearance?"

Once again, Nick thought about Jonathan and why he had heard nothing. And, as always, he wondered about Joanne and whether she really cared. "Perhaps they have, but the Russians have chosen to ignore the fuss."

"But why this pretence that you are someone else, that you are the person the CIA pretended you were?"

"Perhaps it was a real personality, that of a real black-marketeer, and I'm being punished for his sins."

"And where is he now?"

"Perhaps he's dead."

"And where does the CIA think you are? And where does your bank think you are?"

"I don't know!" Nick's voice was rising again. And where do Jonathan and Joanne think he is?

"Is there someone who wants you to disappear? Were you sent on a mission by the CIA that was a trap? To make you disappear?"

"I keep trying to persuade myself that is impossible...."

"Come on, let's go back to work. We'll think about it."

CHAPTER 24

MORE DIGGING

The next day there was no mortar waiting for them, and there was a great wind tearing across the building site. The old man got them moving. First, he sent men across the site to fetch materials. That meant they picked up any scraps they could find for the fire. Next, he and Mikhail went looking and returned with several sheets of hardboard. These they pinned across the open walls to keep out the fiercest gusts of wind.

They lit the fire and clustered around it. The Armenian said, "All we need now is a bottle of brandy and we're as cosy as bugs in a rug."

The old man took Nick out of earshot of the others and started with some excitement. "I don't think you have told me everything. We must go over it all again. One possibility is that the Russians didn't want you to meet your brother."

"But why let me come at all? Why give me a visa?"

"Perhaps they didn't realise who you were until you were in the country."

"That's possible. I didn't request a Visitor's Visa as this can take up to six months to obtain, and also I didn't want to prejudice my work for the bank."

"Or your work for the CIA."

"So I planned to complete my work and then take a trip to my brother's town. I had already asked for travel arrangements to be made to go down to Rostov."

"Rostov? Is that where your family comes from?"

"Yes, Rostov on Don. The port on the Sea of Azov, just off the Black Sea. Right down South. Well, that's where he lives now."

"About a million miles from here."

"So maybe they didn't like that when they discovered what you planned, together with your false identity."

"Why put me here? Why not just stop me? Why not arrest me in my real name? Why this farce? It's as though they want to punish me or make me disappear."

"Maybe that's it. Maybe someone wanted to punish you or make you disappear."

"But who? And for what?"

"Only you know that. Think back to your past."

"Well, my mother was an emigre, and she may have left enemies."

Nick was reluctant to go further until he had explored who Kilgas was.

"Perhaps there are enemies of your family who have been waiting for revenge, and they are now in positions of power. When they discover who you are, they seize this opportunity to get even."

"It's possible, but it seems so unlikely." Nick pulled the flaps on his cap lower and tried to tuck them into the collar of his worn jacket. The wind had started to whistle through the bones of the power house structure. The old man then had a severe coughing fit and waved Nick's help away. They moved round a corner to get even further out of the wind.

"There is one fantastic theory I have had which doesn't seem at all possible. It involves the bank in London, but I don't see how they...."

"Tell me about it anyway."

"During my last few months at the bank, I uncovered what appeared to be some gigantic frauds. If I was right, then there is someone in the bank who would have wanted me to disappear."

"Who knew about what you had found?"

"Two people involved in the frauds. Neither too scrupulous."

Nick told him about his discoveries in Spain and later in Mexico.

"Who knew about your suspicions in the bank?"

"No one. Well, no one who could have been involved. I had mentioned my suspicions to one of my closest colleagues, but he wasn't even in the bank when most of these frauds were organised."

"But could he have told someone?"

"Not at all likely. He is a true blue Englishman, good family and so on."

"Weren't your friends Burgess and McLean true blue...?

"And then I told my boss, who told me it would be investigated by a specialist, and I was taken off the case."

"So your boss knew of your suspicions?"

Nick continued, "And he had informed his contact in the CIA."

"Who was the man who found the information on your brother? And who organised your task in Russia?"

Nick wondered, as he had done so many times in the past, whether Jonathan could have, even perhaps without meaning, told someone, and whether Mike Carmina...?

"But even if that were the case, how would they persuade the KGB to pick me up and put me here? None of it makes sense, except if it were all a terrible mistake."

"It's not a mistake. It sounds to me as though the ignoring of your true identity is quite deliberate and planned. No mistake there."

They had come round full circle again, just as Nick had on

his own so many times in the past. But this time he was a little clearer that there was a plot of some kind, and he was foolish to wait and hope for the eventual discovery of a mistake.

"Not only that," continued the old man, clearly enjoying using his brain on this mystery, "but someone back in England, perhaps even your bosses, must have wondered where you were, what happened to you, and therefore someone here must have developed a cover story of some kind that was acceptable to them over there."

"What do you mean?"

"For example, that you were killed in an automobile accident and your body so badly burned that it was unrecognisable?"

Nick nodded slowly.

"And something like that would need to be fairly well arranged."

"So, let's suppose that whoever was organising the fraud in the bank realised that you were on to him and also knew that you were coming to the Soviet Union.."

"Or arranged it."

"Yes, or arranged it. Had contacts sufficiently powerful here to be able to organise your disappearance and the cover story."

"That would presuppose that whoever it was here also had an interest in the fraud or an interest in my disappearance."

"All of which I agree, my young friend, is highly unlikely, but then everything in the world of the nineteen seventies looks highly unlikely to me. Come on, the mortar has finally arrived, so let's get back to the real world."

Nick noticed that the old man had difficulty rising, and throughout the rest of the day was not his sprightly self.

CHAPTER 25

THE OLD MAN
UNCOVERED

It was soon after the old man started to lose his strength that he began to want to talk to Nick about his past.

"I am old, Nikolai, and to my surprise, getting older."

"How old are you?"

"I was thirty when I was first taken into Russia. What does that make me?"

"When were you first taken into Russia? What do you mean, taken into Russia?"

"I am not Russian."

"Well, that's not surprising. Most people here are not Russians. Lithuanians, Latvians, Georgians, Ukrainians, Poles. I heard that you were a Cossack." Nick held his breath.

"Well, I'm not. I'm German."

"Your name is Alexander?"

"In Germany and in Russia."

Nick was disappointed. He'd been hoping to hear something about the Cossacks. "German? But how the hell did you get in here? And why did anyone think that you were a Cossack?"

"Oh, everyone knows that I'm not a stupid Cossack. I'm just known as that because I came into Russia as a Cossack at the end of the war."

Nick had to calm his voice. "When exactly?"

"In 1946." The old man looked pensive.

"1946. And you were thirty. You've been in here for thirty-nine years." The thought of it depressed them both. "That makes you sixty-nine. Sixty-nine! How have you survived this long?"

"I don't know how. But I know why."

Nick waited.

"Revenge. I just had to get my revenge. And I now begin to realise that perhaps I never will."

"Revenge on whom?"

"Revenge on this Goddam system that locks hundreds of thousands of good men away and murders millions. And revenge on one man in particular. The man who put me in here. And the man who had hundreds, if not thousands, of Cossack officers killed."

"When? Where was this? Were you at..?" Nick couldn't formulate the question he wanted to ask.

"Let me tell you how it happened, how I came to be locked away here. I am a German army officer. In escaping from the advancing Allies, I made the big mistake of taking the identity of a Russian who had fled Russia and fought against the Russians on the side of the Germans. I thought these people would be looked upon with sympathy by the Allies. After all, they were the first opponents of the Communist state."

"Why were you ashamed of being a German?"

"I know what Germany did during the war. I was a good soldier. I did my job extremely well."

The old man was choosing his words with care. It was as if this was his one chance of explaining himself, what he was and what had happened to him. No one had ever wanted to listen to his story before, and he had lost all hope of the story meaning anything to anyone.

"Because I was so good, I was promoted to be the personal assistant of a man who was not so good. A man who condoned, then encouraged, and finally organised atrocities in his attempts to gain further promotion in the Nazi regime. Although I was personally never involved in these atrocities, I knew about them, and I was mortified by them."

Nick wondered how true these excuses were; he had seen how ruthless the old man could be, but why should he seek to justify himself to Nick? He no longer had anything further to gain or to lose – except perhaps Nick's good opinion of him. But he must know that good opinion of him was limited to the direct experiences in the camp.

"But why do you want to know about all this?" He was probing to find what audience he was addressing.

"I am interested in the history of what happened at the end of the war." That was a little weak. "And I want to know what makes you what you are. I am not sure I really understand you at all."

The old man grunted with acceptance and was about to start again when Nick went on, "There is another reason, a very personal reason."

The old man looked surprised and puzzled.

"My mother was a Cossack."

"You told me she was Russian."

"She was a Cossack. Her husband and her father fought with the Cossack regiments alongside the German army against the Russian army."

The old man was silent for a minute. "I did not know this. What happened at the end of the war?"

"I am not too sure, and I have no one to tell me."

"Your mother?"

"She died. In London. A few months before I came on my visit to Russia. She never told me anything about the past. Some people don't."

"I know how she felt."

"But she left some papers. They told me a lot about her childhood and about the war, but the ending was confusing. She was in this huge refugee camp in Lienz run by the British. They were all handed over back to the Russians. She got away. She was helped by a Scottish doctor."

"And your father?"

"Yes, he was my father."

"He was your father? But what about your mother's husband and her father?"

"I don't know. I think they went back to Russia."

"Where was this?"

"In the Drau Valley, in Austria."

"I was at the Drau Valley. At the very end. It was terrible. What were their names?"

"Korshunov. My grandfather was Gregor Korshunov."

The old man looked severe. "He was a great man."

"You knew him?"

"Everyone knew him. He was the most stable force around. He did all the negotiations with the British. He blamed himself for what happened. He trusted the British. He admired them. He thought he was on their side and they on his. And they betrayed him. He persuaded the Cossacks that it would all be alright."

"I am not sure I understand."

"I am not sure anyone does... He was handed back to the Russians. Along with Nikolai Zharkov."

"Alexei's father...."

"They were interrogated by the General. Genera Koshevoi."

"Koshevoi? Not Misha Koshevoi?"

"Yes. Misha Koshevoi. They were both taken outside. And shot."

"Shot?"

"Yes, I saw them being shot."

The wind whistled across the flat icebound landscape, and both men shivered almost out of habit. Nick placed a cloth-wrapped hand in front of his face to relieve it of the force of the biting wind for a moment.

He had difficulty absorbing this information.

"You knew Koshevoi?"

Nick muttered, "He was once my grand-father's best friend."

"His best friend?"

"When they were very young."

He gasped in disbelief, "My grand-father's best friend had my grandfather and my mother's first husband... shot!"

The old man described the hell that was the Drau Valley some forty years before: The uncertainty, the waiting, the confusion, the panics, the rows of tents, the scrambling horses, the food shortages, all made worse by the mixed nature of the camp inhabitants.

CHAPTER 26

TOWARDS THE END

Nick discovered later that the old man had not had to accept him. As the dominant team leader at that time he could have chosen who he wanted. He must have seen a challenge in this poor young man determined to do himself harm. Or perhaps he saw some mindless compassion that might be harnessed at a later date when he might need it.

Now the old man had become really old. And the Rat, who had done deals with the old man in the past, who had kept him sweet when he was king of the heap, now had started to torment him, and Nick was the old man's only support.

Before the old man's long decline in power had begun, he had taken Nick in hand and taught him how to survive.

"Don't fight the system. Exploit it while you can," he said with a smile. When Nick wanted to stand up for his rights, the old man knocked him down. "You have no rights, no rights. All you have is a stomach that needs more food than it is getting and a body that needs fewer beatings than it is getting. You clearly have no mind, or if you do, you do not use it."

The old man had had a team who were totally loyal to him in return for his ability to obtain more food and easier work and the odd concession from the Rat or one of the other guards.

"The Rat is a large man of low intellect who wants nothing more than a quiet life," explained the old man.

"He appears to be more like a sadist who can't wait until his next beating."

"That, my young friend, is where you're wrong. Because he beats, you think he enjoys beating; he looks forward to it. This is not so. He beats because he is afraid."

"Afraid?"

"Yes, afraid. He is afraid what will happen if he stops beating."

"But he doesn't beat you."

"That is because he is afraid what will happen if he tries."

Nick had heard the story of the guard whose body had been found with barbed wire wrapped around the throat the night after he had had a go at the old man. It was an old story, but it was still alive and the old man did nothing to discourage it.

"But I am growing old, and he grows less afraid. But I also said that he likes an easy life. And so, if every time he deals with us he finishes up having an easier life than before, then he will like dealing with us."

"But that sounds like currying favour to me."

The old man smiled. "You remind me of something I read a long time ago. Something very funny. But I cannot remember what it was." He shook his head, still smiling. "You are definitely not a Russian. Or a Pole, or a Ukrainian, or any of the other dozens of nationalities around here."

Now the Rat was on his way to torment the old man again. He stopped at the end of the old man's bed. "What's the matter with him? Can't he put his trousers on himself any longer? He might need to go back to the lock-up to learn."

Nick kept his head down and thrust the old man's stiff leg into his wadded trousers. The old man coughed violently.

The Rat went on to plague someone else.

The old man was weaker this morning, and Nick thought about taking him to the sick bay after breakfast before the assembly for work. As they left the barrack room in Hut 8 the cold made them gasp. They pulled their collars up higher and held their heads low. They saw the orderlies carrying the barrel of nightsoil away. Searchlights swept the camp, and the lights around the perimeter were still on. The deep snow creaked under their boots, and the cold wind bit into their faces.

They walked past the rows of long huts, grey-white, frozen to the ground. The old man stopped every so often to recover his strength. Nick cursed him as every delay meant that the relative warmth of the mess hall was further away.

They passed the thermometer hanging in a central spot. Nick heard someone curse. "The fucking thing says twenty-nine – I don't believe it." That was minus twenty-nine, not cold enough to stop work; that only happened at minus forty-one. But then, as the old man said, "Your blood froze in your veins."

An early worker, sent to scrub the guard room, was trying to raise water from the well, but his bucket barely fit through the hole left in the thick covering of ice, and his rope was as stiff as a wire hawser.

The mess hall was already crowded. Teams sat at the same table or waited in the aisles for a table to come free. Men were delegated from each team to queue for the food and bring it to the others. The queues were a brawling, shouting scramble as men fought for the scraps that had to sustain them for the day.

Nick found their team's table and saw Fetiukov struggling back with the bowls of skilly. Nick helped him the last few yards and banged the bowls down around the team rapidly before the last of the steam stopped rising. They all plunged in greedily, each with their own spoon, homemade or stolen. They ate fast because they were hungry, but not too fast because they wanted to savour the moment and make it last as long as possible. There were few moments when they experienced anything approaching pleasure during their waking hours, and this was the first of those, so they tried to prolong it for more than the five to ten minutes they were allowed by the waiting gangs.

The skilly was vegetable soup with a little fish. The vegetables were hard to distinguish, but Nick had identified a carrot and, on good days, he had even had a few small potatoes. The fish were small, and the flesh had been boiled off. They sucked at the bones and crunched the heads and the smaller bones with their few remaining teeth. Nick had lost several of his during a severe bout of scurvy two years earlier.

CHAPTER 27

ESCAPE PLAN

Nick had been allowed to visit the old man once, and that had been the previous day. The clinic hut was windowless and stiflingly hot. The so-called nurse was feeding the fire and swabbing the floor. Groans and calls for help were ignored. There was little the nurse could have done for them. Nick walked the length of the long room. The beds were soiled and unmade, and dark blank eyes stared hopelessly from each one. The old man, in contrast, was looking almost cheerful.

"Come to share my warmth, have you? Pull up a chair. Have you brought some chocolates?"

Nick found it hard to join in.

"What is the diagnosis?"

"Diagnosis? They don't know the word."

Then he switched to English. "Look, we haven't much time. We must talk fast."

Nick looked around nervously. They had never spoken English in public before.

"Don't worry. None of these is about to rush out and call a guard. And anyway, by tomorrow it won't matter."

"Tomorrow?"

"Tomorrow I'll be dead. I won't survive another night in here. And tomorrow night you escape."

Nick was astonished. "Escape?"

"Yes. I've planned it all."

And he proceeded to tell Nick in his usual meticulous, detailed fashion his plan for the escape.

"And then you will use Viktor's two-week leave pass and his travel warrant to get to Rostov."

"Rostov. Rostov-on-Don?"

"Where your brother lives. And from then on it's up to you."

Nick's mind was whirling. Adrenalin was charging through his body for the first time in the camps. He had thousands of questions.

"Why would Viktor want to do this?"

"He would rather spend the two weeks with his lover in Angara than with his aunt in Rostov."

"Is that all?"

"He knows I won't tell his superiors about his lover."

"And that's all?"

"That's all in the short term."

"And in the long term?"

"I told him that you would help him get out."

"Out? Out of here? Isn't he helping me get out?"

"Out to the West."

"Out to the West."

"With his lover."

"With his lover. Out to the West. He is hoping that I will help him get out to the West with his lover?"

"Yes."

"Why does he think I can do that?"

"I told him about the money."

"Money. What money?"

"The Swiss bank account."

Nick recalled the conversation about the Swiss bank account. It had taken place just a few days before the old man had fallen ill.

It turned out that in the last few days of the Reich, Colonel Redl, the personal assistant to the infamous Adolf Eichmann, the head of the Gestapo's Jewish Extermination Department, had helped his superior establish bank accounts in Switzerland and had helped him transfer to them all the various parts of his stolen wealth.

"I created one account, and I know how to gain access to it."

"And Eichmann?"

"Eichmann escaped. He spent five years hiding in Germany and Italy. And then, in 1950, ran away to Buenos Aires, Argentina. He was hunted by a small band of Israelis, who tracked him down and captured him in 1960."

"And then?"

"He was smuggled to Jerusalem to stand trial."

"And…"

The old man looked away. "He was executed by hanging on 1 June 1962."

"And no one else knew anything about that bank account."

"Hadn't he used it? And how much is there?"

"He had other bank accounts. And I'd set this one up with passwords that only I knew. And he needed to have supporting documents that I had kept and hidden. So he would have to use it with my help."

Nick's banker's mind went into action. "Can you pass on the passwords? And provide access to the critical documents?"

"I probably could…."

Nick wondered how much had been hidden. "There has been some inflation since the war. Money is no longer worth what it was."

"I know what inflation is. I lived through inflation. I remember the shopkeepers repricing all their goods every morning."

"Well, how much was there?"

"About one million."

"Of what? Deutschmarks? They are not worth much today. A new German currency was created at the end of the war."

"No, not Deutschmarks. Swiss francs. What's that worth?"

"In 1945, probably about $250,000 dollars."

"And today?"

"Well, when I was still working, and then snatched, in 1975, if they managed to achieve a growth rate of about eight percent, and inflation was sometimes as much as that, it was probably worth about four million dollars."

"And now, in 1985?"

"Well, if it kept growing at that rate, and exchange held up, it could be worth twenty million Swiss Francs, or seven to eight million dollars."

"It sounds like a small fortune to me."

"It's not a small fortune. But it is enough to live comfortably. How was it to be invested?"

"The bankers were given investment discretion."

"That could mean they have either blown the lot away or used it to dump all their bad investments."

"I thought the Swiss were financially astute."

"They are. For themselves. The Swiss know how to make money for themselves out of others' fortunes."

The old man looked disturbed and unhappy.

"Don't worry. I'm probably being unfair. They have probably had it all in unimaginative bonds, earning an average of five percent and taking a nice half percent themselves as an annual fee."

"And inflation?"

"If they've kept it in Swiss francs, they have possibly just beaten inflation and it has more than maintained real value."

Nick thought it more likely that as the bank realised the fund was dormant, they had plundered it to boost their more public investments. Not actually withdrawn funds, but placed good performers to the account of active funds with a high profile and allocated the poor performers to the old man's account.

"Why should the account still be there?"

"It was opened on the understanding that there might be

no activity for a number of years. Eichmann foresaw himself having to keep a low profile for a number of years."

"Not, however, as low as it turned out, nor for as many years as this."

"Not as many as this."

Nick looked at the old man on his death bed and wondered once again at the extraordinary man he was. "I remember the Swiss bank account."

And the old man told him in precise detail how to gain access to the account, and where and how to obtain the documents.

"Surely they will need a signature?"

"No signature. The knowledge of the numbers and passwords, and the documents alone gives you access. But you will need to answer some questions. You will need to visit the bank to establish first contact."

"I'm absolutely flabbergasted at all this planning. But anyway, you're not going to die."

At this, the old man broke into a fit of painful coughing. When he'd stopped and had spat the grey phlegm into the filthy pan by his bed, he smiled weakly and said, "I'd better. And when you get out, I want you to find that swine Kharkov for me."

Nick felt a hand on his arm. The nurse was standing there angry.

"I will. I'll find him for you."

CHAPTER 28

GOODBYE AND ESCAPE

The night was dark and quiet. Nick climbed down from his bunk and walked the length of the barracks, holding his valenki in his hands. He had slept with all his clothes on. He knew several eyes were watching him and hoped that the zeks would keep quiet until the night was over. He knew that there were several who would trade the information for extra food or any favour, but he was gambling on the average zek's reluctance to disturb the night. If anyone reported anything during the night, the likely outcome was that the entire barracks would be paraded out in the cold. So when anyone stirred in the night, the information was kept until morning when it was offered around for a trade.

Nick opened the door and slipped out before the cold draught hit too many sleeping faces and woke them. It was early spring, and the thick snow had thawed and seeped through the crust of the earth, turning it into a primeval swamp. A late frost had then turned the yard to concrete. Nick pulled on his valenki and carefully made his way along the side of the barracks.

The air was deadly still and a heavy fog glowed white around the camp. The sound of his boots scraping on the frozen mud appeared to echo into the fog. He heard the muffled, sleepy voices of guards exchanging greetings as though from far away. Noise did not carry in the fog.

The morgue hut was not guarded, and the door was unlocked. Nick entered and closed the door behind him. The place was pitch black and he didn't know where anything was. He felt his way slowly across the room until he reached a long worktop. On it he found the three bodies securely trussed in canvas bags. Two of them were being shipped back to their families. One, the old man's, was to be disposed of locally.

He felt the first bundle, found the wrists, and found nothing on them. The second had free wrists, but on the third he felt the wire wristlet that the old man had asked him to wind around his arm as he lay in the hospital and outlined the plan.

He pulled out his sharpened spoon and cut the cord at the head, and then pulled it free down the length of the body. He felt the body and cursed as he realised the guards had left it with only a thin shirt and trousers. In the dark, Nick struggled to undress the old man's body. He discovered that it is almost impossible to take upper garments off a stiff body with its arms folded across its chest. After half an hour of struggle, he had managed to switch clothing with the corpse. He kept the cap, the heavy coat and the valenki for the time being, but he realised that he would have to sacrifice them in time. He was sweating heavily, and he felt the moisture on his back turn clammy and begin to freeze in the icebox-like hut.

He laid the body out on the floor and went back to the now empty body bag. At the bottom of the bag, he found three large rocks. He took the largest and carried it across to the old man's body.

He was glad that he could see nothing as he carefully raised the rock and brought it down on the old man's face, smashing it beyond recognition. He gulped and then gritted his teeth. His desperate need to complete the plan for the escape fought with his feelings of sorrow and guilt as he looked at the old man's remains.

There was no blood on the rock, but he needed to wipe it clean of tissue and pieces of bone before he replaced it.

The old man's body was thin and light, and Nick was able to raise it onto his shoulder before he left the morgue. It was still dark outside, and the fog still clamped down the sound as Nick staggered across the gaps between the barracks to the mess. He laid the body against the wall under the window to the stockroom. He removed his valenki and pulled them onto the corpse's legs. He put his cap on the head and tucked the flaps into the collar. Last of all, and with reluctance, he pulled off his coat and put it on the corpse. The night was lightening, and he saw the patch with his number on the shoulder as he ran away.

The cold from the frozen ground was coming through the rags wrapped around his feet, and the freezing fog was biting into his chest. Nick hoped that the guards would assume that he had been caught and killed by an urka when he was about to steal some food. No one would be too surprised at his murder now that the old man's protection was finally completely removed. There would be little investigation, and the drunk doctor would not take too much time examining the corpse covered in frozen frost.

The morgue was even colder than outside, and Nick knew that he would have a long, cold wait until the morning. He searched the dark, cold hut and found a worn blanket. With this wrapped around him, he strode up and down the small hut in an attempt to keep warm.

As the morning light weakly penetrated the fog he climbed into the body bag, laced the cord through the old holes, pulled it tight and tied it firmly. He hoped that no one would notice that it was tied on the inside. He stifled his mounting claustrophobia and tried to breathe slowly and deeply. He tried to think of calming thoughts, but found them hard to find. His mind kept coming back to the closeness of the bag, to the blackness, to what was going to happen in the morning. The cold penetrated the hut, penetrated the bag, and he shuddered as he thought of the old man lying outside, dead and battered. He shuddered again as he felt the stiff canvas rub against his cheeks, and he thought of the old man's face, stiff and dead.

The long-frozen camp waited still in the arctic night, thousands of bodies lying in unquiet sleep, tortured in their dreams, not wishing to hope, but hoping only to survive the night so they could survive the next day. And Nick wondered whether he could or would do either. Was this the end, or was this the beginning? He could not imagine life outside. He did not think that he could cope. He felt more fear than he had felt all his time in the camp. The camp he had come to learn to cope with. He wished the old man was with him. He needed his advice and guidance. But then he thought that the old man would know even less about the outside world than he did, and he would not have been of much use. The old man had done more than enough for him. His death had been his last gesture.

Nick had seen the old man negotiating with the young guard called Viktor and had wondered what the deal was this time. The old man had little left to deal with, but he still managed to continue to strike deals, although they became smaller and smaller.

Then the old man's health had suddenly deteriorated sharply, and he had been taken into what stood in for a hospital. It had beds, and it had a large stove that was kept burning well. There was a doctor and a small supply of drugs, but the main work was done by a trustee, a thermometer, and aspirins. No one was too interested in unproductive labourers, and once a body entered the clinic, it was to leave a few days later either to go back to work or to go to the morgue.

CHAPTER 29

FINAL MOVES – CAMP

When they came for the bodies in the morning, Nick wasn't worried about finding anyone. He was worried once more about surviving the day ahead.

The doors crashed open, and Nick saw the chinks of light through the seams of the body bag. His body was cold, very cold, and he did not have to try to keep still. His breathing was shallow and soft. His whole body appeared to be in a semi-coma. He was stiff, and he made no attempt to flex his joints. He dozed and thought of the old man dead and lying in his bed and in his body bag.

He heard, as though a long way away, the two guards arguing about the task ahead. They finally agreed to take the old man's body to be dumped first and then to take the others to the railway station at Angara. They also agreed to carry his body on the plank on which he lay because this would make their task easier in some way.

He heard the truck being reversed up to the morgue hut, and he switched right off as he was carried and lowered into the truck. The soldiers cursed the weight of the rocks in the body bag. The bumpy ride soon loosened him up, and he felt the first surge of excitement as he heard the shouts of acknowledgment as they passed through the entrance gate. The ride then seemed to go on for nearly two hours, and the truck made heavy weather of it, gears grinding as they pulled up long uphill climbs and swinging from side to side as they tore down curving passes.

Finally, they came to a stop, and he heard the guards get out and have a smoke. More loud arguments were then followed by the truck being slowly and carefully reversed. It stopped, and he heard the guard climbing in. He felt the head of his plank being slowly raised, and he thought they were going to slide him out of the truck. When the drop came, he was taken completely by surprise. One second he was jerked up into the air, and the next he was flying and tumbling out and down. He screamed silently, gritted his teeth and clutched his sharpened spoon.

The rocks hit the ice first and went straight through, tearing his body after them through the hole and into the black icy depths of the lake. Lake Baikal is the deepest lake in the world, and Nick's terrified mind visualised the dark unending depths beneath him as he plummeted down and struggled and tore at the body bag with his spoon. The water rushed into the bag and numbed him even further. Panic tore over him as he felt that he could not get out. Then the spoon slashed a cord, and he felt the bag begin to open. He lashed out again and again and became tangled in the cord as he forced his body out.

At last, the stones pulled the bag down away from him, and he came clear and started to claw his way back up to the surface. Bubbles ripped out of his mouth as the air expanded in his lungs as he neared the surface. He saw the ice before he hit it and then panicked again as he searched for air and for a break in the ice.

The ice was thin after the earlier spring thaw, and he came through screaming for air, lungs gasping and grunting in great gulps of life.

The lake's surface was black and quiet, and as he hauled himself towards the shore he heard, far above, the sound of a truck engine pulling away. He had to get to solid earth before he froze up completely. Already he had no feeling in his hands, and he saw mysteriously that one was bleeding. He saw a long branch ahead of him and tried to grab it, but his hands could not hold on. Every time he half climbed out onto the ice, it cracked and collapsed beneath him. He felt hope fading and consciousness go just as an arm surrounded him and dragged him clear.

PART THREE

CHAPTER 30

GETTING OUT

Nick woke as the slap swung his head to one side. Another slap swung it back. He realised that someone was slapping him hard from one side to the other. He was being held forward by his shirt and thumped. He began to get angry and tried to swing his arms in self-defence.

"Come on! Wake up! You can't fall asleep now!" Whack.

"Oright. I'm awake," he mumbled through frozen lips. Then he saw and felt the fire. It was a small fire, but it was slowly getting through to him. He felt his face begin to crack, and the unbearable pain as the feeling slowly came back to his feet and hands.

"We have to move soon. We cannot stay here." The man was rubbing Nick's hands and legs to get the blood moving again.

"I want to stay. I am in love with this fire."

The man chuckled. "All relationships must end sometime." He was a man in his early fifties, with a grizzled face, white hair and a large paunch.

In spite of his belly, he appeared to be fit and strong as he helped Nick up and then half pushed, half dragged him up the face of the small earthen cliff leading up from the lake.

Nick saw, as in a dream, the gnarled black roots of the trees that struggled to hold on to the face of the cliff. He grabbed at them like a drowning sailor grabbing at the rungs of a ladder up the side of a rescuing oil tanker. He looked up and through the twisted black branches, he could see the sky. The sky, bright and glowing in the mid-morning light, was the best sky he had ever seen. The blood moving through his veins made him feel warm through the cold, and he found he couldn't focus on the ground ahead.

He nearly fainted, and the white-haired man held him on the cliff face and shouted, "Get on!" He wasn't used to looking at things like this. He could see the colours in the earth, the small buds on the branches and, above, he saw again the blue, blue of the sky. He was used to seeing the grey of the man's clothing ahead, the grey of the barrack hut, the grey of the biting wind, the grey of despair. Now he was blinded by the bright blue of hope.

At the top of the cliff, Nick saw a large rocky space where vehicles stopped to take in the view or to throw out the garbage.

"My van is just down the road." The white-haired man staggered into the brush, half carrying Nick. They found the van, and Nick was bundled into the back and covered with several blankets.

"I don't know how you survived. It's a miracle, a miracle," the man kept repeating. Nick wanted to tell him that he wasn't yet sure that he had survived, but as the little van's heater started to work, he fell asleep.

He woke as they pulled up outside an 'izba', the local little log houses. Nick asked, "Is this where Viktor's girlfriend lives?"

The white-haired man chuckled. "I suppose you could say that."

"I understood," Nick persisted, "that I was to go to the house of Viktor's girlfriend."

"Friend."

"What?"

"Friend. I am his friend. My name is Yevgeni. Come in before someone sees us."

Realisation, rather late, dawned on Nick. Slightly embarrassed, he followed into the small house and was immediately impressed by the tidiness and neatness. There was a log fire burning, and he went straight to bed.

When he woke up, Yevgeni had a hot bowl of soup, which he served with a broad grin. "My soup is the best in Siberia. Viktor says it is wonderful."

It was wonderful. The best soup he'd had for ten years. Nick fell asleep again.

"What work do you do, Yevgeni?"

"I am a baker. I bake the best bread in Siberia. It is wonderful. Here, you have a piece. Today is my day off. Tomorrow I must work. Then it is Saturday and Viktor is coming, and I am making him the best and biggest cake in Siberia."

Then, as an afterthought, "You must catch the train on Saturday. Viktor's ticket is for Saturday. You must get well and strong by then. Have some more of my wonderful soup." He grinned with delight and excitement.

Viktor arrived at midday on Saturday and looked critically at Nick and his condition.

"You must leave today. The ticket must be used. You cannot go later." Viktor was very nervous.

"I am much better than I was. I am stronger. I am walking."

"You look terrible. You look one hundred years old with a broken, scarred face. But all zeks look terrible. They will see straight away what you are, and then we will all be caught. Why did I ever agree to this crazy scheme?"

"It will be alright," Yevgeni calmed with his broad grin. "Nikolai is a brave man. He will behave perfectly. He is strong. He has eaten lots of my soup. It is..."

"... The best in Siberia. Yes, we know. But that face, that hair, he looks terrible. He looks twice as old as you."

They argued like an old married couple about how to make Nick look better. They fed Nick some more soup and bread. He gobbled it up.

"The train leaves from Angara station at three o'clock to catch the Trans-Siberian Express leaving Irkutsk at eight fifty-five this evening. Viktor will deliver you to Angara station at two-thirty, and he will see you on to the train. But after that, it is up to you."

"What happened at the camp?"

"What do you mean?"

"What happened about the bodies? I mean, does anyone suspect? Are we alright?"

"Of course we are alright. They found your body and you are lying in the morgue right now. Your funeral takes place at the lake tomorrow morning. No one suspects anything."

"You are nervous about something."

"Of course I am nervous. I am nervous about everything. I am breaking all the regulations I can, and I know exactly how bad the conditions are where I can finish up. And all for what? For two weeks with this fat baker."

Yevgeni grinned. "He is always like this, nervous as a kitten. He will be better when he has eaten some of my...."

"Oh! Be quiet! We must go over all the instructions." Viktor then went over all the occasions when Nick would be asked for his papers, and how he must behave on the train. He would be travelling second class, which meant that he would be sharing sleeping accommodation with three others, some of whom could be female. He would be expected to be sociable, but could pretend to be tired and go to sleep. There would be a toilet with a wash hand basin at the end of each corridor. A car conductor would look after each coach. He would need to tip the conductor so much and not too much.

"Money! What will I do about money?"

"Here are one hundred roubles. They will more than see you there."

"How can I thank or repay you?" One hundred roubles was about one hundred pounds, a great deal of money to a guard in Russia.

"No need. The old man passed on more than that to me in the way of information before he went. I am making a profit." For the first time, he laughed and clapped Yevgeni on the back. "And don't forget, when you get out, you will come back for us." He laughed again, jumped up and did a little dance with Yevgeni. Yevgeni grinned.

"Now," he sat down, serious again, "the train arrives in Moscow three days later at four-forty in the afternoon Moscow time. You will have eaten in the restaurant car, but never taking so long that you make acquaintances. I suggest that you leave immediately on the soonest train to Rostov, which is at ten that evening. The trip to Rostov will take two days. The distance is a great deal shorter, but the train is slower and stops frequently. You may not be able to get a sleeper."

"And you will be met by your brother. Alexei. Don't get more confused."

Nick was almost ready to get excited.

"Your brother will get you on a boat that will sail away from Russia towards Europe. Perhaps Italy."

"How?"

"He is a manipulator. He knows people. He helps people escape. He is trying to organise the creation of a country for the remaining Cossacks. It is futile. But perhaps, one day?"

"But how can I get out of Russia when I have no identity? I am dead?"

"It has been done before."

Nick was nonplussed. He couldn't thank them enough.

Yevgeni packed several cakes and some fruit in a parcel. Nick put on a suit of Viktor's clothes and admired himself in the mirror. He looked and felt better already.

CHAPTER 31

AWAY, AND THE MEETING

The train journey was a mixture of exhalation of freedom and adventure, and the terrifying uncertainty and high possibility of doing things wrong and getting caught. He managed to get away with things, kept his head down, thought carefully of all options before acting, and struck up no relationships and got to know no one; although he was desperate for communication and wanted to tell his tale.

He lurked around at Moscow station and managed to remain unnoticed. He found the train to Rostov, climbed aboard and found a seat. He didn't try to find a sleeper. He found sleeping on a noisy clattering train easier than his experience of the past ten years. He had something to eat, but nowhere enough. But he and hunger were friends.

At Rostov, there was someone waiting to greet him. He almost thought he recognised him. They stared at each other, then moved towards each other, and then hugged. Nick felt very emotional. This was Alexei, his older half-brother. Alexei was born in 1939 to Nick's mother Polya and Nikolai Zharkov. He was forty-six, some eight years older than Nick, and had never left Russia.

They spent the rest of the day and night exchanging stories. Alexei wanted to know why his mother had left him in Russia and gone to England when he was just six years old.

Nick said, "I'm not sure, but your mother Polya and your father Nikolai fought with the Cossack army on the side of the Germans. You were left in the hands of Piotra, our mother's uncle, who apparently cared for you very much as a child."

"They were wonderful parents, or grandparents. But I never found out what...."

"Your father, Nikolai, was a fighter and a leader. Your mother learned to use weapons and to fight. She also learned English and helped as a translator."

"The Cossacks travelled across Russia down to Italy, to Tolmezzo and further. At the end of the war, the Cossacks negotiated with the British as they felt they could trust them. At the infamous Yalta conference between Stalin, Roosevelt, and Churchill, it appears that the Cossacks were 'betrayed' and all the officers and soldiers, including your father, were handed over to the Russians, who wanted revenge for the betrayal in fighting with the Germans."

"Polya was fortunate by being saved through her relationship with the Scottish doctor, Cameron, who befriended her and managed to get her separated from those who were handed over."

"That is your father?"

"Yes, he was my father.

After our mother died, I found many papers containing her descriptions of her experiences of life. And some of her memories of you."

Alexei said, "What did she say?"

"I'll try to recall some of it. She said that in 1938 she married a brave man called Nikolai. A year later she had a son they called Alexei. He was the love of her life, and for a year nothing else mattered to her."

"When Little Alexei was only four he was a beautiful boy. He was dark and quick like his father, had fierce eyebrows and was full of mischief. She cried when she thought about him. She thought she left him in good hands because her uncle Piotra stayed behind, and he and his wife loved Alexei almost as much as their own grandchildren. When she left, they thought it would only be for a short time, and that they would be back, triumphant."

"She also wrote that she could have taken Alexei with her, but it would have been difficult, and she decided it would not have been fair. She never knew whether she made the right decision. Would Alexei have survived all that they later went through? She didn't know. She wondered whether Alexei had a good life? What he is doing? She wondered he knows she exists. She didn't know, didn't know.

She had thought seriously about sending back home for Alexei, when he was nearly five years old and still living with my uncle Piotra and his wife.

She said that Gregor missed little Alexei, he missed that Alexei was. growing up without him, and he may never see him until he is grown up.. she said that Nikolai said nothing, but was always sad.

Our mother fought her way halfway across Europe to stay with her father and her husband because each of them believed that the regime in Russia was wrong.

They were told that in two days' time, May 31st, they would be returned to Russia. Fear and panic swept the camp. They were given a form of comfort by a request that they should pack up all the officers' belongings so that they could be taken to them. This gave them false hope that they were still alive and could use their possessions.

She went to the trouble and heartache of packing Nikolai's boots, uniforms, belts, underclothes, pipes, and so on, with tears in her eyes and despair in her chest. She could not believe that after all they had been through together, the march across what felt like half the world, she would never see them again. But the stories were that families were split up when sent to the camps. she wrote a letter to Nikolai and one to her father. She did not mention Alexei, as she did not know who might read these letters."

Alexei looked at the ground and shuddered. "I never saw my father. There is no record of what happened, or where he was sent, what camp he ended up in."

"Oh! I was hoping that you had grown up with him. Why are you here? Here, in Rostov?"

"I came to search, to find. I found nothing, nothing. Until I found you today." He almost smiled.

"I have heard something." Nick gritted his teeth.

"What have you heard?"

"The man who helped me in the Prison. The man who planned and arranged my escape. Alexander Kilgas."

"What about him?"

"He was at the Drau valley when the Cossacks were handed over to the Russians by the British."

"He saw...?"

"He told me..." Nick gulped. "He told me many officers were tried... by the Russians... and punished."

"Did he see my father?"

"He says he saw Gregor, our grandfather, and...."

"And. And?"

"Your father, Nikolai Zharkov...."

"What? What?"

Nick hesitated, looked at Alexei, and then blurted, "Taken out. Taken out and shot."

Alexie went very silent. He looked at the sky. "I always knew it was possible...."

· · • · ·

Sometime later, Alexei said, "Don't worry, I will get you on a ship that will go through the Black Sea across to Italy.

Was there a future? Would he see Joanne again?

CHAPTER 32

SHIP ESCAPE

Alexei told Nick they would board the cargo boat 'SALVEZZA'. Nick asked, "What does salvezza mean? It sounds as though I am being saved?"

"It does mean saving, but it also means salvation, safety, redemption, or, in this case, anchor. A good name for a ship and, coincidentally, a good name for your situation."

Nick breathed. "Let's hope it works."

"We are boarding as visiting guests to the captain, Captain Antonio. An old friend and someone who knows your problem and is willing to help."

"How can he help?"

"You will stay on board when I leave. He will hide you through-out the journey in a small private cabin that is not used next to his. He will make sure you get enough food delivered to his cabin."

"Who will I be hiding from?"

"The crew. This is a cargo vessel. Sometimes there are one or two passengers. But this time you are the only one."

"How long will the trip last?"

"It is 2,300 nautical miles. You will go through the Sea of

Azov, the Black Sea, the Bosporus Straits, the Sea of Marmara, the Dardanelles, the Aegean, the Sea of Crete, the Ionian Sea, the Adriatic, and then you arrive at Ravenna. The trip will take about ten days."

Nick gasped. "Not an easy journey."

"It will give you time to relax. And recover. Which, I think, you need."

"But what is my identity?"

"I have prepared some simple papers identifying you as 'Nicolas Camarano'. They will be good enough between you and the captain. And they will be sufficient for you to leave the ship at Ravenna. But you will need a new, better identity after that. Anna will create a new identity with convincing documents."

"Anna?"

"Anna Agnelli. Agnelli is based on lamb. It signifies a pious or timid person. Anna is neither. She will meet you at Ravenna. She is an expert at creating identities with supporting documents."

"Is it that easy? Do you trust her?"

Alexei was firm and positive. "She is half Russian. And she has created many identities for refugees. We have worked together several times with success. Easy? Not at all easy. But consider how many have evaded being caught. After the war, Adolf Eichmann hid in Germany, then Italy for five years, and then in Argentina for ten years. Martin Bormann, head of the Nazi Party and secretary to the Fuhrer, escaped to Argentina and was still there in 1974. Others – Klaus Barbie, Josef Mengele, and others. They were all prominent much wanted evil men who were able to hide under false identities. They could do it... so you can do it."

They boarded the ship that afternoon. Captain Antonio was charming, but didn't waste any time. Nick was taken straight to his cabin. Antonio wasn't surprised by the lack of luggage.

Nick and Alexei hugged and promised to meet again if and when they could.

The ship cast off the next morning, and the sea journey commenced.

Nick went on deck at night and shouted his joy and lust for vengeance at the moon and at the harbour lights disappearing in the distance.

Nick found the gentle movement relaxing, and the closed doors of his cabin were not too threatening. He could sleep well on the comfortable bed and mattress, and he could see the sea waves through the small porthole.

Alexei had given him some copies of the local newspapers to read and one book. The book was 'JOURNEY INTO THE WHIRLWIND', published in 1967 by Eugenia Ginzburg, who was accused of terrorism in 1937 and spent eighteen years in labour camps until she was rehabilitated and returned to Moscow. She died in 1977.

Reading the book, Nick was reminded of the terror that he'd experienced, and he realised that many others had experienced the same, and even worse. She survived many dreadful experiences – being stripped and left in a dirty dark cell with rats scuttling around. She survived by creating poetry. Poetry!

One poem read:

> *And I too will sing of joy and suffering*
> *Let the devilish host*
> *Howl and cavort*
> *I have that*
> *Which they have no power to take from me.*

Nick thought he might try poetry, although it was now too late. He should have tried it when inside. He wondered if Joanne liked poetry.

Another document explained how the Gulag system had been ended by Khrushchev in 1960 as he started his process of de-Stalinisation and masses of prisoners were released. But, as Nick could readily confirm, the process remained, and the prisoners, although somewhat fewer, down from over seventeen million to now under one million, were still numerous and were still treated inhumanely and used for penal labour.

The newspapers he was given were enlightening as they told stories of the complicated lively outside world he had forgotten. But none were relevant, except for a tiny piece that looked at the world of finance. Apparently, it appeared that the world was struggling its way out of a severe financial crisis in the early eighties. Many banks had suffered, and many financial businesses had gone bust. How was the City doing? He needed to know more.

He needed to know how his 'colleagues', Lutz, Jonathan, and others, had fared. He wondered, once again, whether the old man's theory was no fantasy and they were participants in his misfortune? Why had no one done anything to save him?

And why had Joanne not searched for him? Why had he heard nothing?

CHAPTER 33

ITALY

Nick was concerned and sceptical about the idea of some Italian girl called Anna being responsible for his entry into Italy and his new identity and papers.

Anna came on board and was taken to Nick's cabin for them to meet. When he was greeted by Anna, his concerns were not diminished. She was a flamboyant, rather exotic lady dressed to be noticed and admired. Not someone he felt could be relied on to do this tricky task.

She asked immediately to see his papers drawn up by Alexei. She liked what she saw, but felt they were not sufficient. She had prepared some papers herself and proceeded to combine elements from both sets.

As he heard Anna work and describe what needed to be done, Nick's apprehensions started to melt away. He decided that although her appearance was Italian, her approach to the difficult task was Russian, dour, solid, and focused on results.

They left the ship, together with the crew that was not needed for the unloading. Passport control was an unnecessary show. He fitted in with the crew and was even more poorly dressed. And Anna knew everyone and nodded and smiled as she wafted through.

Her flat was nearby, and she showed him his bed, made some coffee, and launched straight into discussing his new identity.

She liked 'Nicolas Camarano' and would like to build on that. But Nick was not keen. "It is too close to my real name, Nicholas Cameron, and too easy to set off a suspicion."

"We will develop a new name."

Nick thought a Russian name would be more convincing as a financier in London. "What about a Russian name?"

Anna wondered. "I have a name we could use – Nicolai Chamov. That is the name of my uncle who came to Italy to see me one year ago. And died."

"Nikolai Chamov? Are you sure?"

"I have his papers. I have not reported his death in Russia."

"OH! Why?"

"I am still receiving his income. He had retired. He had no family. You could take over his identity with ease. I can change all the papers. And we will need new photographs. Of that face."

"This sounds too good to be true. I'll think about it."

"Let's have dinner. I'll cook my lasagne. And we can start now with a glass of the best red wine." She poured two glasses, raised her glass and said, "Salute."

They had a great dinner. Nick loved it. "This lasagne is the best lasagne I have eaten for ten years."

"When did you last eat a lasagne?"

"About eleven years ago."

Anna laughed. And then seriously tried to fill Nick in with what had happened to the world in the last ten years.

They had a few more laughs. Nick was relieved that his first contact with a woman for many years was amusing, enjoyable, and involved interesting discussions. She was attractive, but he tried to ignore that and concentrated on re-entering the real world and solving his identity issues.

CHAPTER 34

SWISS BANK

Nick rang the Swiss bank and was treated like a potential criminal. He spent some time laying out his details and explaining that he wanted to talk about a particular account. He was told that he needed to come to the Head Office and bring his identity documents.

Anna had his identity documents ready and said that a trip to Switzerland would be a dramatic test of their credibility. No one gets into Switzerland easily.

Nick remembered a personal experience when he went skiing in Switzerland as a young man. He had forgotten his passport and was ushered swiftly into a small office and interrogated. He was asked whether he had any documents that could support his claims of identity. As a joke he had pulled out his ski pass from the previous year and showed that. "Ah! A Swiss document! That is proof enough that you have travelled here before, and we will allow you in."

Anna told him to forget his ski pass. He could use his new documents in the name of Nikolai Chamov. They would work. And they did.

Nick went straight to St. Moritz, which was just over the

border from Italy, and which was now developing into the top ski resort. It has deep roots in the sport. Its Corviglia mountain is considered the birthplace of winter sports – and winter tourism. In 1944, the Grand Hotel in St. Moritz was burned out in a tragic blaze. It was now being rebuilt, and Nick was able to talk his way in to see the original remains. He found his way to the large room on the top floor overlooking the mountains and the slopes.

A safety box remained embedded in the wall behind the doors. Nick used the passcode, opened the box and found the papers that would enable him to access the bank account. He left the building and hurried to the centre of St. Moritz, where there were several banks. He found the one he needed.

. . • . .

At the bank, Nikolai had to hand over his identity documents and then explain why and how he could have access to this particular account. Nick explained his close relationship to Kilgas, who had created the account, who was now dead, and how he had been passed the access codes and information. Eventually, he felt secure enough to disclose the codes. And he handed over the relevant hidden documents. To his surprise, they were accepted.

He was given access to the account. And he saw that it had grown from the initial one million Swiss francs to one hundred million US dollars. Half was in a bank account, earning interest. The other half was invested in a variety of global stocks and other investments.

Nick was given a chequebook and immediate access to the funds. He chose to keep the funds invested in the same manner, but asked to be kept informed daily on the funds' performance and to be involved in any critical decision-making.

He then astonished the bank by asking for support in creating a charitable fund to help refugees, particularly refugees from Russia.

Nick returned to Italy, travelling first class on a train. He met Anna and asked her to identify properties for sale that he could view.

Two months later, he viewed a large farmhouse in Monteriggioni. Monteriggioni is a medieval walled town located on a natural hillock, built by the Sienese in 1214 as a front line in their wars against Florence by assuming command of the Via Cassia running through the Val d'Elsa and Val Staggia to the west.

It is a small town, almost a village, surrounded by a solid stone wall on its hilltop. Two towers, one a church, the other a fort, at either end of a road that climbs the hill and then motors through, past the cafes and the main piazza. Stone houses with tiled roofs cluster around the road and the various side alleys. Most of the wall can be walked around, with spectacular views of the surrounding rolling Tuscan countryside, iconic lines of cypress trees, and the San Gemignani towers.

Nick fell for the large rambling farmhouse on the outskirts of the village. It had red brick tile floors, tiled roofs in red, large dark beams, wooden windows opening inwards, dark green shutters opening outwards, old heavy furniture, chickens running around the garden, helper Dino turning up on his Piaggio Ape, a motorcycle driven little van, a garden with mixed olive and fruit trees, three cats, an old tractor, and wonderful views of the Tuscan hills.

He bought it and moved in.

Anna initially refused to move in with him, but eventually did so. She always avoided developing a relationship with those she helped escape and develop a new identity. But with Nick it was different. She listened to his stories and felt an overwhelming sympathy for his situation. She felt his need for understanding and help, and she decided that she really wanted to help. She insisted on calling him the 'Count of Monteriggioni'.

And Nick, against all his reasoning, found that her company and advice became desirable and almost irresistible. They grew closer and closer until Nick also found her physically desirable and irresistible.

The contrast between the depressing nights in the dark, damp, dirty, dangerous cells and the evenings of pleasure in a soft, cosy bed with a loving companion was overwhelming.

But he still thought of Joanne, where she was, what she was doing, and whether she still remembered him.

CHAPTER 34B

Uncovering the Truth

Nick told Anna about the tragedy at the end of the war. How the Cossacks had been handed back to the Russians by the British and the dreadful results.

Anna nodded knowingly. "I have heard a little of this before. Other escapees have told similar stories. Your brother is a brave man carrying on trying to help people leave Russia."

Nick asked, "What did they think about the British and the way they acted."

Anna grimaced. "They were disgusted. Disgusted. They cannot believe the lovely British could be so inhuman."

Nick shook his head in shame. "No, no, it does not seem possible."

Anna added, "And there are some facts I discovered. About who was involved."

"Who was that?"

Anna searched for some papers. She dragged some out and leafed through them. "It says here that the man in charge of all the situations was a Field Marshal Alexander?"

Nick nodded. "Yes, I think that is correct."

"The man who gave the orders was an officer on the staff

of the General who made the decision. His name was Harold Macmillan."

"What? Harold Macmillan!!" Nick was astonished by this piece of information.

Anna nodded vigorously. "Yes. Yes. And this document says he was later...."

"He was... our Prime Minister! Let me read that document!"

Anna carefully and slowly handed it to him. Nick grabbed it and searched. And then he read:

"There were 70,000 Cossacks and Yugoslav Ustashi in the British zone of Austria, where Toby Low was the departing chief-of-staff to Field Marshal Alexander. Under Harold Macmillan's orders, Alexander turned over all the Soviets and Yugoslavs, despite his doubts about 11,000 women and children, to a slaughter that began almost immediately."

Nick was completely silent. Then, "How could he do that? How could he live with himself? How could he become Prime Minister? Which he was from 1957 to 1963. Would we have voted for him if we'd known all the facts?"

More depressed silence. Anna searched the papers again. "It says here that MacMillan was ashamed of his decision for the rest of his life. It was a tough decision to make."

Then another document: "Macmillan was also the minister advising General Keightley of V Corps, the senior Allied commander in Austria responsible for Operation Keelhaul, which included the forced repatriation of up to 70,000 prisoners of war to the Soviet Union and Josip Broz Tito's Yugoslavia in 1945. The deportations and Macmillan's involvement later became a source of controversy because of the harsh treatment meted out to Nazi collaborators and anti-partisans by the receiving countries."

Nick was appalled, embarrassed and ashamed. He thought again of what his mother must have gone through. And how incredibly lucky she was to have formed a relationship with that Scottish doctor who took her away and saved her life.

Anna got up and slowly came over to him, and then gave him a long, consoling and loving hug. She really cared.

"I know so well how you are feeling." Anna stroked his back.

Nick looked at her. "Why? From other escapees you have helped?"

Anna shook her head and looked very sad. "No. Worse than that."

Nick questioned, "Why worse? And why have you got into this task of helping escapees?"

Anna turned away. "My father... escaped."

Nick tried to express sympathy. "Oh! When was that? Why did he escape?"

Anna gulped and continued, "That was before I was born. He escaped from the gulag. After many years inside."

"What? How was he when he got out?"

Anna shook. "Very, very bad. He only just survived. But he was full of fight. He met my mother, which he said really saved him."

Nick said, "Where is he now?"

Anna almost sobbed. "He died when I was fifteen."

Nick grabbed her hands. "How sad."

Anna let go and walked to look out of the window at the lines of trees on the skyline. "He never really recovered from the gulag."

Nick tried to be quiet. "Is that what drove you...?"

Anna reluctantly said, "Yes. I met other escapees, and gradually learned, and became obsessed by the entire process."

Nick persevered. "Was your father a Cossack?"

Anna muttered, "No, Nicolas... He... was Ukrainian."

"Ukrainian? Why was he in the gulag?"

Anna tried to explain, "Ukraine was part of the Soviet Empire, but it is a separate country. The Cossacks were not the only people to fight the Bolsheviks."

Nick remembered the old man telling him. "*As the German army began to retreat out of the Ukraine, the White Russian regiments retreated with them. One was composed mainly of Ukrainians and another a Cossack horde."*

Nick confirmed. "Yes, I remember I heard that they also fought on the side of the Germans in the war, as did the Cossacks."

"And," Anna stated forcefully, "they also were handed over to the Russians as prisoners of war being 'returned to their home country'."

"Oh, my god!" Nick stood up. "Cossacks were not the only ones!"

Anna nodded again. "And so that is why I have devoted my time and efforts to trying to help people escape from Russia."

Nick queried, "And your mother?"

Anna laughed. "My mother thinks I am crazy. I am wasting my life. She thinks I should get married, have a child, and devote myself to my art."

"Your art?"

Anna tried to be modest. "I paint. You haven't looked at the paintings on the walls here. You haven't commented."

Nick stared around at the walls of the room they were in. "I have been amazed by the variety and quantity of different pictures you have on all your walls. They are all yours?"

Anna looked down. "Well, not all. But nearly all."

"They are wonderful. They tell the story of Tuscany better than da Vinci or Michelangelo."

Anna laughed. "No, not that good."

"Where did you learn?"

Anna tried again to be modest. "I taught myself. But I do a lot of painting at a studio in a nearby village. A wonderful studio, put together by an English sculptor in old disused buildings. He now has studio rooms, rooms people can rent to stay in, with bathrooms, and a café/restaurant on the outside terrace. It is wonderful. And I meet a lot of other artists there."

"Perhaps you can take me one day."

CHAPTER 35

EVENTS IN THE CITY

Nick needed to find out what had happened in the financial world since he had disappeared. He wondered what had happened since the dramatic fall of more than fifty percent in the market from the 1972 high to the year before he left. He saw that there had been a more dramatic recovery. The market had grown by more than four times from 1975 to 1985. The clever lads who had survived the 1975 crash had more than prospered since.

He also wondered what had happened to his 'colleagues' and 'friends'. To his astonishment, he uncovered that three of them had founded a new investment company, FINCO, at the bottom of the crash and had ridden the huge wave with tremendous success. They were now among the largest financial companies in London.

The three were Lutz, Carmina, and his gentleman friend, Jonathan. Jonathan was now an MP and the chairman of FINCO, Lutz the CEO, and Carmina was on the board of directors.

The company had been launched with several millions of pounds in investment. Nick wondered where the huge sums had come from. He suspected he knew where some of the funds had shamefully come from. But not all. There must be other big money behind it.

He needed help to investigate, and he wouldn't and couldn't approach these three. He sought the help of an old friend from university he had known and trusted in the past, who now worked as a freelance dealer. He was young, not so young now, enthusiastic, and completely honest and reliable. As a result, he was not progressing very far or very fast. But he had clients who needed someone they could rely on and trust. Paul Trainor. Nick found his number and rang him and left a message. He gave his name Nikolai Chamov and spoke slowly with a Russian accent.

When Paul rang back, he was clearly very cautious. Nick explained that he knew nothing of the share markets and needed careful, trustworthy advice before he moved into investing. Paul asked for personal details and wanted to know how much they were considering investing. Nick explained that he was a Russian who was now resident in Italy. He would supply all the finance details when and if they could meet. Paul was very interested, but made no attempt to force him into revealing too much.

"I have been reading a little about a company called FIN-CO. Perhaps you could tell me something about it and whether it is a good investment?"

"Of course. That should not be a problem. I will send our fee structure to you."

Paul then also sent Nick a roughly written summary of FINCO's history:

1978 Launched as a financial boutique in preparation for the liberalisation of the financial markets. Founding shareholders were defectors from American Bank: Frank Lutz, Jonathan King and one ex-US government employee: Mike Carmina.

1979–83 The group owns a small merchant bank, has invested in a number of small industrial companies, and built up a

· small conglomerate concentrating mainly on printing and publishing interests. Participates in and leads the destruction of the print unions by moving printing plants out of Fleet Street and taking up new technology. Appears to have no shortage of funds to invest. Its shareholders are not well known. A large block of shares is held by a Lichtenstein Trust.

1983 The company goes public and becomes a PLC. The share issue is massively oversubscribed and doubles in price in its first year.

1983 FINCO bids for and acquires the Daily Reflector, the ailing but sole surviving left-wing newspaper. Using the new technology and facing down the unions to reduce costs and lowering the standards of the paper by increasing the number of semi-nude girls and the outrageousness of some of its reporting.

1984 Finco acquires major publishing groups in Germany and France. The German acquisition is completed only after the old family owner suddenly and inexplicably removes his opposition to the purchase. Once again, funds seemed to be easy to obtain, although by now, with the share flying high, new issues of shares at high P.E.s can be used to finance almost any acquisition.

1985 Finco acquires a major British insurance company, hawk Fidelity, with significant operations in the USA.
Finco acquires one of Britain's largest conglomerates, containing international businesses in tobacco, brewing, hotels and restaurants. Finco rationalises everything it buys very rapidly, selling those operations that are not attractive and tightening financial and operating controls in those it keeps.

Reported profits rise dramatically year on year, but because of the rapidly changing nature of the group, it is difficult for financial analysts to determine to what extent the group is actually obtaining higher profits from its acquisitions.

Paul then added, "But the market in 1987 is beginning to crash. And FINCO is very vulnerable right now. They need support."

Nick now had a plan on how to enter the world of FINCO.

In the 1987 crash, FINCO shares suffer badly along with all other previously overrated shares. They are then bought heavily by a mysterious European group operating under nominee names through Swiss banks. FINCO nearly goes under when fresh funds suddenly and surprisingly become available.

A European investment group called COUNT has made a small fortune through its investment at the bottom of the market and is now one of the major shareholders in FINCO.

CHAPTER 36

FINCO

Deep in the heart of the City of London is a small cobbled courtyard with two plane trees and a statue of Sir Gerald Cornwallis, a former Lord Mayor of London. He stands arrogantly, with one leg forward and one hand on a walking stick, his nose slightly in the air, and his general air of confident assertion only slightly damaged by the long white streaks left by the resident pigeons.

The buildings that surround the courtyard are small four-storey Georgian houses with discreet but smart front doors. The general noise of the rushing workers of the City fails to penetrate the narrow entrance, and the presence of one of the two major financial centres of the world within a few yards is disclosed only by the National Westminster Tower, which can be seen looming over one end of the yard. The north side of the yard is the pleasanter side as the sun reaches most of the windows for most of the day. Most of the doors are locked and remain locked. The very end one has a small discreet brass plaque with the name of the company that occupies all the buildings on the north side – FINCO.

The top floor is across all the buildings joined together

and is occupied by three very comfortable offices and a small boardroom. The boardroom is occupied by an executive committee meeting which is being chaired by Jonathan King, MP He is preparing for a press conference to be held later that afternoon.

"So it's agreed that I should start with a summary of the company's history, concentrating on the past four years since we went public in 1983. I will remind those present of the company's early history when it put together a series of spectacular deals across Europe, and when it had the ability to attract supporting funds from investors who wished to remain anonymous."

"Why bring that up?" The speaker was a huge American in an expensive double-breasted suit with a long unlit cigar waving in one hand. He no longer wore his hair in a crewcut, but it was still very short on his large skull, and it was now snow white.

"Because if I don't, Mike, someone else will. And I would like to get it out of the way on my terms."

"No, I wouldn't invite it." This was the third member of the meeting, another American, but smaller, with a pasty face and glasses with thick lenses, thicker than they were ten years earlier. "Keep it out. No one's interested in the past. They're all excited about the deal that's hot right now. You just skate over the early years to give them a feel of the successes. They will all be waiting to hear the latest. If anyone wants to waste our time raking over cold coals, he will be shouted down by our friends in the press. I think we have a lot of faithful followers right now."

"Alright, I'll leave it out." Jonathan slowly drew a line through some of the early lines of his draft. "But don't think we can totally avoid the issue."

"Big deal? Don't you call this a big deal? We will be climbing out of this recession, doubling our size and perhaps joining the top 500 companies in Europe." Carmina waved a box of matches dangerously close to the long cigar.

Jonathan frowned at the cigar and continued, "FINCO is announcing a bid for BAP, one of the top five British multinational industrials. We are confident that this acquisition will make FINCO's future even more interesting and successful. FINCO will be more than doubling in size and joining the top 500 companies in Europe."

Lutz tries to calm things down. "That will interest large investors. We are nearly there."

Jonathan holds up one hand. "But we are still short of several hundred million."

Carmina points a jabbing finger. "Why is our usual investor holding back?"

"He feels he is already too open to discovery. But we have another very interested investor."

Carmina leans forward. "Who is that?"

"They do not want to be identified. They are a very successful investment company that has made a small fortune in the latest market moves while the market crashed. The investing vehicle is called – COUNT."

"COUNT?"

"Yes. There is a rumour that the man controlling the investments considers himself an Italian count, or Conte. But there are few Italian contes. And his name is Chamov, Nikolai Chamov."

Carmina was concerned. "That sounds Russian."

"He is a Russian. But now lives in Italy. And considers himself Italian."

Lutz said, "Not another Russian! We have trouble enough."

"Trouble? Without our Russian, we would never have launched."

Carmina was cautious. "Keep that within these closed doors. He is a substantial investor, but we have not publicised his involvement. We do not want to be torn apart because of that!"

Lutz said, "I understand he has used his profits to buy a

couple of very luxurious houses and is seeking to buy a football club."

Carmina warns. "We do not want questions. But does our first Russian know the second one?"

Jonathan is firm. "We have not informed either one about the other."

Lutz said, "Well, meet with Charm-off, or whatever he's called, and let us know whether we can get his involvement and the necessary funds."

"We have a meeting planned for next week. Apparently, he is coming to London for the first time. It needs to be very private. Paul Trainor, who some of you may have dealt with, has provided the introduction."

CHAPTER 37

REVENGE?

Nick was desperate to find the truth of the events that surrounded, and perhaps caused, his disappearance into the gulags.

Did he want revenge? There were moments when all he felt he wanted was total unforgiving revenge. But he needed to find the truth before he allowed his desperate desire for revenge to be satisfied.

He searched for advice. He read about revenge. He found quotes:

"A man that studieth revenge keeps his own wounds green."

"Revenge is a kind of wild justice."
> *Francis Bacon: Of Revenge, 1561–1626*

"Revenge proves its own executioner."
> *John Ford: The Broken Heart, 1586–1639*

"Revenge triumphs over death; love slights it; honour aspireth to it; grief flieth to it."
> *Francis Bacon: Of Death*

"If you prick us, do we not bleed? If you tickle us, do we not laugh? If you poison us, do we not die? And, if you wrong us, shall we not revenge?"

Merchant of Venice III

"If you wrong us, shall we not revenge?" Did they wrong me? Which of them did the wrongs? And if they did, shall I revenge? And does continually studying revenge keep my wounds green? Would I be better to ignore and forget? I should, if revenge is its own executioner.

And where does Joanne come into the story? What role did she play? How involved was she? Does she know anything at all about what went on? Will he ever find out? Why does he keep remembering her shouting, "Don't go, don't go. I'll never see you again."

Did she know something?

Nick shook off his enveloping concerns and started packing and preparing for his trip to London.

Anna was not happy that he was going, but she assured him that his papers would stand up to scrutiny.

"Conte Nikolai, you will be careful, no? Stai attento. Sei molto importante per me. Ty ochen' vazhen dlya menya."

. . . . .

Nick entered London in a daze, overwhelmed by the memories. Everything looked the same, and yet nothing looked the same. He was slowly surprised by the number of small changes that affected life. Harold Wilson had been the Labour Prime minister in 1975. Now Margaret Thatcher had taken over the Conservative party and had become the first female leader, and was now the first female Prime Minister. But Elizabeth was still the Queen.

The population of London had declined as more people sought employment and housing elsewhere. The population had fallen from over eight million to under seven million. The cars had changed. He hardly saw any of his own most popular car – a Ford Cortina. But, surprisingly, he saw a Mercedes', and a Land Rover.

A senior representative of the investment company, COUNT, is invited to London to meet the Directors. Paul arranged a meeting for Mr. Chamov to meet with the directors of FINCO.

He had steadied himself for the meeting by walking slowly through the City. He saw the anxious hurrying young traders rushing past and remembered his keenness in the old days. He remembered when he had been full of ambition and drive, when a deal a day had been necessary for self-respect, and when insider trading was one of the perks of any unscrupulous investment manager.

He and Paul found the grand doors of FINCO in a Georgian building in a small courtyard. The headquarters of the powerful conglomerate was announced discreetly with a small brass plaque. The meeting room had a large view of St. Pauls from across the Thames that Nick recognised as a Tintoretto. The armchair was the usual plump buttoned leather merchant banker type, but the carpet looked old and threadbare enough to be really valuable.

A tray was brought in with a pot of coffee and cups of the thinnest white porcelain. There were several copies of FINCO's Annual Report stacked neatly on a coffee table. Nick had a well-thumbed copy in his office, and he knew it by heart. Nick opened a crisp copy of *The Financial Times* while he waited, and soon found the article on the FINCO bid for the BAP Corporation in the middle of a market crash. Jonathan's smooth, pleasant face beamed out at him from a publicity photograph.

The article covered all the known points of the deal, the audacity of this financial conglomerate that was taking on one of the top three British multinational industrial companies, the plan to unbundle, etc.

· · • · ·

Nick was completely calm when they walked in. They did not recognise him. Jonathan King walked in first, followed closely behind by Frank Lutz. Neither of them showed any signs of recognising Nick at that stage. It was not surprising, as Nick's appearance had changed dramatically. His hair was a salty grey and very thin on top. His face was scarred and ravaged. His skin had yellowed with tiredness and age. His teeth were bright and new. His short beard was mottled grey and spoke decrepitude, not elegance. His frame was gaunt and thin. He had not managed to rebuild, and he walked with a serious limp.

It was only much later in the discussions that Jonathan knitted his brows and asked in that familiar friendly, quiet spoken manner, "Tell me, Mr. Chamov, have we ever met before?"

Nick looked back and tried to smile. "If we have, I am sure we would remember?" The Russian accent helped convince Jonathan.

Jonathan shook his head and looked puzzled.

Lutz had started the meeting with caution. "Mr. Chamov, we understand that COUNT is a major investor in FINCO, and you would like to be involved in FINCO's future growth opportunities, but would like your participation to be treated with utmost discretion?"

"Yes, I am new to this investment business and would like to be guided by experts."

"We understand you have already had some successful investments?"

Nick showed embarrassment. "I have been very lucky so far. I cannot claim success, only very good fortune. And I am aware that this might not always continue."

Paul offered, "Not all just good luck?"

Jonathan was kind and helpful. "We may be able to offer you the opportunity of being one of the major investors in the launching of our new major corporation. As you may have already been informed, or read, we are about to launch a very large bid for one of Britain's largest companies?"

Nick showed innocence and ignorance. "Yes, I was told something. But what does that mean, 'one of the major investors'? Perhaps you could outline the details of the opportunity."

Jonathan was cautious. "The acquisition is hotly contested. We shall benefit, and succeed, if we have the continued purchase of our shares by some secret investors."

Nick asked with enthusiasm, "You would like our support by our buying your shares during your acquisition?"

"Well, you have already shown support, and we would like this to continue to grow. The market is currently very difficult. Which offers opportunities, but also dangers."

Nick showed more enthusiasm. "We have many other investment opportunities. But of course we can do that, can't we, Paul? We shall operate out of Europe."

Paul nodded.

"We shall organise this with our partners and bankers in Switzerland. We, and some friendly associates, could buy twenty percent of your company."

Paul hesitated. "But we may be asked to obtain an indemnity should the acquisition fail."

Jonathan looked uncertain and turned to his two partners for agreement.

Lutz blustered, "Of course, we shall do that. No problem. Would you like another coffee?"

CHAPTER 38

REGATHERING

Two weeks after the submission, and the examination of all the information and figures to do with the coming major financial deal, Nick was invited to a drink and talk event to mix with the directors, other investors, and interested parties. The event was to be held in the In and Out Club on Piccadilly, where, oddly enough, Nick and Jonathan had enjoyed many games of squash some years ago. The In and Out was not known for its squash court, but was respected as a venue for this kind of event.

Nick had never felt comfortable at 'events'. He was never sociably lively, and his experiences over the past ten years had not changed that. His introverted character perhaps had always preferred meetings in twos or threes. He particularly remembered one awkward 'event' held in the US Embassy in Grosvenor Square that had, in many ways, changed parts of his life.

Tentatively, he handed his coat in and walked into the large gathering of wild talkers. The room was an old imitation of a banqueting hall. It was too bright, too crowded, and too noisy. Too many people and too many glasses of too expensive drinks.

He knew no one. Or no one he could admit to knowing, although he recognised a few faces.

Jonathan greeted him, found him a glass of something, and introduced him to some serious participants without mentioning his likely involvement in the coming deal. They had agreed to keep it under cover.

Nick asked questions about how London was developing and explained his Italian residence. Some questions were asked about Italy, Tuscany, the villages, and art. He mumbled knowledgeably about how wonderful it all was.

Then he saw her across the room. She was as attractive as ever. But her clothes were now exotic and fashionable. She was, understandably, no longer the young, art-loving, left-wing rebel. He wondered whether he should approach. He decided to watch and wait. He had already had the shocking, but not surprising, news that she was married to Jonathan, and they had children.

He avoided Lutz and Carmina, and was busy describing Casole's charming village when Jonathan approached him and said, "Mr. Chamov, I would like you to meet my good lady wife, Joanna. Joanna, this is one of our new associates, Mr. Chamov."

Nick gulped and almost dropped his drink, then slowly turned and saw Joanne. She wasn't really looking at him; like most people he met, she tried to avoid looking at the heavy scars. She just held out a limp hand to shake and gave a limp smile.

They exchanged some pleasantries. She fingered what looked like a very expensive necklace, looked bored, and scanned the room as he and Jonathan exchanged banalities. Then Jonathan got called away to meet someone of greater importance, and Joanne turned to try to give him more polite attention.

They spoke at the same time. She started, "What do you...." against his, "Do you enjoy...." She stopped and looked at him encouragingly. Nick said softly, without the Russian accent, "You go first...."

She froze and mumbled slowly, "No... You... go... first..." And then looked straight into his eyes properly for the first time. And froze again.

They stood for a few minutes, just staring. Then Nick asked, "Joanne, do you have a family?"

She gulped and pulled herself together. "Joanna, I'm known as Joanna. And yes, I have two children."

"Are they a lot of work and trouble?"

She hesitated again and looked around as though for help.

Joanne was more than puzzled. She hesitated, but then eventually said, "Mr. Chamov, you almost remind me... of someone...."

• Nick was very wary. "Oh?"

Joanne answered very carefully, "No, no, it's just a friend... An important friend. From many years ago. Much younger than you."

Nick remained quiet and drank.

Joanne said, "Sadly, he died... in a car crash... in Moscow."

Nick gulped again.

The situation was salvaged by Lutz barging in. "Joanna, you have met the amazing Russian Italian now, have you? We think we may be able to do some useful work together."

Joanne was almost speechless. "Oh! ... good..."

"Mr. Chamov, I must introduce you to another of our directors, Mr. Carmina. Carmina, this is Mr. Chamov, who we have been telling you about."

Nick kept his Russian accent as deep as possible. "Mr. Carmina, it is a pleasure to meet you."

They shook hands, and Carmina looked at Nick as though investigating an archaeological dig. "What part of Russia are you from, Mr. Charm-off?"

"Many different parts. But recently from Rostov."

"Rostov? Isn't that where the Cossacks are from?"

Nick shrugged. "I believe... there is some claim of that kind."

"So you are not a Cossack yourself?" Carmina laughed,

and they all laughed.

Nick needed another drink, and almost wished he was back in a gulag.

Joanne nodded, backed away, and left to talk with another lady.

CHAPTER 39

THE PARK

Notting Hill is a pretty grotty part of London. Holland Park is the pleasanter, more elegant part of Notting Hill. Nick knew that Jonathan had a grand house in Holland Park. Later that week, Nick went to the park in Holland Park. He knew it from the past. He had always enjoyed the contrast between the wilder, wooded parts of the park with the more cultured and flowered lawn parts. And he admired the elegant remains of Holland House.

The park also contained a sports field and an outdoor children's adventure playground. Nick walked past the playground. He saw Joanne sitting with a book on a park bench, with an expensive-looking handbag next to her. She was watching children playing on the equipment slides and climbs.

Eventually, Nick approached Joanne and stood by her. She didn't turn. He sat down next to her.

"I wondered when...." she said without looking.

Nick wondered what to say. "Is that one of your..."

Joanne interrupted, "How did you..." and stopped.

They looked at each other.

Nick said, "You go first...."

Joanne said, "No! YOU go first...."

They both nearly smiled and barely laughed.

He saw a young boy climbing enthusiastically where he himself had climbed as a young child.

"Is that one of your children?"

"That's my son."

"How old is he?"

"Seven. Here he comes."

"Mummy, I want a ball. I want to play football."

"Nicky, there are no balls here. Here, you climb and slide. The football is on the other field."

Nick gasped. "Nicky?? He's called Nicky?"

"His name is Nicholas, but everyone calls him Nicky."

"Nicky, say hello to my friend, Mr. Chamov."

Nicky examined the stranger shyly. "Hello, Mr. Chamov."

"My name is Nikolai, so you can call me Nick, or Nicky..."

It was Joanne's turn to gasp. But Nicky liked it. "Nicky too, hello Mr. Nicky too." They both laughed. And Nicky ran away, back to the slides, and talked to an older girl. Who then came towards them.

Nick stiffened and asked, "Is that your daughter?"

"YES. That is MY daughter."

"She's very brave and athletic."

Joanne nodded. "Yes, she is. She is very active, successful at school, and loves her daddy."

"She looks older."

"Yes, she is."

"How old?"

"She is eleven."

Nick froze and gulped. He thought to himself – Eleven!!?

"You look surprised."

"No. I'm sorry, I didn't mean... What is her name?"

Joanne pondered. "She is called Pollyanna. Everyone calls her Polly."

Nick was completely astonished. He shook and couldn't

speak. He looked around the park, which seemed to be almost spinning.

Joanne asked, "Do you have any children?"

"No. Er, I don't think so..."

She looked closely at him. "I think I know."

Nick said, "I don't. I want to ask a thousand questions."

"So do I. Maybe another time. I'm being picked up in a few minutes."

"In that glossy luxury limousine? The preferred transport for an art lover, a left-wing rebel?"

Joanne shook her head, not at all embarrassed.

Nick stood and started to walk away. "Another time, then. Another time."

Joanne said, "We must. We must."

A pheasant walked shyly up towards them. It pecked the ground, hoping for breadcrumbs, then turned and opened up its glorious tail feathers.

Nick looked across at the playground. "She is lovely...."

Just then, Polly came running over to her mummy. "Mummy, I want a drink."

Joanne took a bottle out of her handbag and offered it to Polly, who drank in gulps.

"Polly, say hello to my friend, Nikolai?"

"Nikolai? Like little Nicky? Hello Nikolai. Goodbye. I'm going back to the swings."

"Goodbye."

Nick turned and walked slowly away past the pheasant without looking back.

When he did look back, Joanne was staring at the ground, shaking. She mopped her eyes as her chest heaved.

CHAPTER 40

DIGGING

Nick needed to know whether anyone had been involved in his abduction eleven years earlier. And he needed to know whether the FINCO operation was entirely respectable and legitimate.

He met again with Paul and began to explore these issues. He gradually discovered that Paul was an avid investigator. It wasn't just financial analysis and digging that captivated him. It emerged that he loved crime mystery stories and was forever imagining plots and plans behind all events in life.

"Paul, we need to understand the true story behind FINCO, its development and the facts behind all the sources of funds."

"I have already discovered that they have hidden companies and bank accounts in several offshore locations."

"Where? How have you uncovered this?"

"St. Vincent, the Grenadines, Cyprus, Monaco, Belize, the Virgin Islands, you name it. They are funnelling funds for several Eastern European oligarchs – Ukraine, Azerbaijan, Kyrgyzstan, and, of course... Russia." Paul gave Nick a knowing, questioning look.

He continued, "Wealthy people want to keep their funds hidden from their government. Especially wealthy Russians. Like you?"

Nick did not rise to the suggestion.

Paul carried on, "But I think I have identified the fact that perhaps you are not Russian?"

Nick ignored that suggestion. "What Russians have you uncovered?"

"Well, it's a little staggering. But there is one important initial investor who helped create this enterprise, who may be Russian."

"May be...?"

"The responsible individual remains hidden. All that can be seen is that the company providing the funds is registered in Cyprus. It is called Tatarsk."

Nick was astonished. "Tatarsk!!?"

"Yes, do you know the name?"

Tatarsk was the name of the village where his mother had said his family came from. Nick answered very slowly, "Well, it may be the name of a village in Russia...."

"So?"

"So, I think you should definitely continue to examine who is involved in that company." He became fiercer. "I need to know! Where are the company's headquarters?"

"They have no offices in Britain. They do have the frequent use of a lawyer's office. I believe they communicate with FIN-CO through that office."

"Do we know much about those lawyers?"

Paul was confident. "Strutt & Symonds. They act for FIN-CO in all their corporate activities. But possibly also in many of their strange offshore activities."

"What else can you find out?" Nick needed all he could get.

"I can have the offices watched and monitored for any visiting clients."

A few days later, Paul reported, "We have noted several Russians entering those offices for meetings. We have managed to track some of the names. One especially, who arrives in a Bentley and is treated like a visiting Lord."

Nick stood up and asked eagerly, "Do you have his name?"

"No, he is Russian, and he has left the country. Gone to Luxembourg."

"And something else," said Paul. "The directors of FINCO are all flying off to Luxembourg tomorrow."

"Let's follow them. See who they meet." Nick was getting eager.

They kept a low profile in Luxemburg, but were able to follow Jonathan and Lutz to a central office where they were to meet with someone to make their final decisions.

They saw a car draw up, and someone got out and walked to the office doors.

"That's him. That's the man who came to the lawyers' offices."

"Could you ask the driver what the man's name is?"

Paul wandered over and chatted. He came back and said, "Koshevoi. Koshevoi. I think that's how you pronounce it?"

Nick collapsed back and banged his head as he fell.

Paul leapt forward. "Are you alright?"

Nick mumbled, "I'm OK. I'm OK." He got up slowly. "Are you certain it was Koshevoi?"

"Yes. Koshevoi. General Koshevoi. You recognise the name?"

"I'm afraid I do."

They investigated and discovered that he was a high ranking officer of the KGB. He was the son of old General Misha Koshevoi.

CHAPTER 41

THE LAUNCH

The directors took the bait and went for the big acquisition. Their move was large and public. The acquisition was hotly contested and could only succeed if secret purchases were made of the target company's shares. The Count had agreed to arrange this with his partners and bankers in Switzerland, but only if he was indemnified should the deal turn sour. He assured them he would arrange for the purchase of twenty percent of the company by friendly but undisclosed associates.

Nick was invited to the launch of the deal but asked to sit quietly at the back. It was a private launch, with just FINCO's directors plus some invited investors and senior staff. It was an indoor paneled room with closed windows and a large screen.

Coffee was offered, and iced buckets of champagne lurked, waiting.

The tension was noticeable, but also in the air was an expectation of joyous success and celebration. Jonathan came over to comfort him. "We think it would be best if you remained quiet and anonymous. No one should think you are part of our triumph. So we advise you to keep your head down and don't shout with joy."

Nick nodded vigorously and tried to appear willing and subservient.

Jonathan persevered, "We believe this success is just part of our normal story and do not want it to appear as something extraordinary and unusual, which, of course, it is, thanks to investors like you."

Nick was humble. "Of course, of course. This is your triumph, your success, that demonstrates the wonderful enterprise that you have built. I am just a fortunate innocent participator, not the creator. I will be glad to be a quiet beneficiary of your remarkable creation."

"Thank you, thank you." Jonathan was now being kind. "We shall bring you many other significant opportunities in the future. I'm sorry, I must leave you to your coffee, as I must talk to some of the other investors. I hope you will join us soon for a glass of champagne?"

"Yes, yes, I would be delighted." Nick laughed to himself.

The large screen at the front of the room showed the state of the market and had some news items covering the launch and bid that was about to be announced.

He saw Joanne enter, walk up to friends, and studiously ignore him.

The process began with a dramatic self-congratulatory speech by Lutz, followed by a more modest, humble, but glorifying one by Jonathan. Nick huddled further back and kept his very low profile.

The screen blazed into light, and the launch and acquisition was announced. The share price had shot up overnight in anticipation, from 80 to over 100. It then grew fairly dramatically to 120, then 130, and faces were all wreathed in smiles of joy and success. Bottles of champagne were already being opened and gently offered to a few.

Time flew by, and the share price continued to climb, but ever more gently. It then hesitated at a point, at 150. Nick noticed that Lutz began to look concerned. Lutz had projected that, with COUNT's support, the price should reach the necessary 200.

It froze at 152, and more than Lutz began to look worried. Nick shrunk down even further. He wondered whether Paul was up to managing the buying and selling of shares. He wondered whether his plan could or would succeed.

Then came the collapse. The price slowly began to drop, to 140, then 130. When it reached 121, Lutz started searching the room for Mr. Chamov. Nick moved his seat behind a glamorous green tall plant. He noticed that some of the leaves were withering and turning brown. It needed watering; it needed support.

Lutz found Nick and asked roughly, "Chamov, what's going on? What's wrong?"

Nick took his time. "I think it just needs watering. It hasn't had all the support it should have had."

"What the hell are you talking about?"

"This poor plant has not been given the attention it deserved."

"For Christ's sake, man. The share price is DOWN, DOWN. What are you guys doing about it??"

Nick looked at the screen. "You're right, you're right. It's now back down to 105! And collapsing fast. This is a disaster. I'm going to lose my shirt!"

He saw people leaving the room. "Where are they going?"

Lutz despaired. "They've lost all confidence. They're probably leaving to sell before they lose it all. Are your guys buying?? As YOU PROMISED?"

Nick shrugged his shoulders. And hoped that Paul had already shorted the deal as much as he could. And continued to short.

Lutz got aggressive. "YOU are losing a fortune. You have to step up and save the deal."

Nick tried to look afraid and embarrassed. "I shall have to go and see what is happening in our dealing room. It is just next door."

"I'll come with you."

"No. We are not supposed to be acting together. I don't think it would be wise for you to be seen in our office."

Nick slipped out and went next door. He found Paul frantic on several phones. "Have you shorted enough?" he asked Paul, who could hardly look up.

"Yes, we've sold all our shares and sold masses more. The whole strategy is being successful. The price is now below 80! And still collapsing."

"I think they all borrowed heavily to be big beneficiaries of this deal. Some of them must already be nearly bankrupt. I'll go back in."

When he entered the room, he saw that almost everyone had left, and the three 'friends' were huddled over, shouting at each other.

Lutz ran over to Nick. "Well? What have you done?"

Nick said in despair. "We've sold everything. It's the only way we can survive. The entire event is a disaster. I think I'm walking out."

And he did.

CHAPTER 42

SNAP

Nick had bought only a small percentage of shares, and he now started selling the shares he had and going short of the rest. This ensured that the acquisition was a catastrophic failure. FINCO's reputation was destroyed, and it made huge financial losses.

The Count's Swiss company publicised its determination to obtain its indemnity. The giving of an indemnity is illegal, the Board of FINCO was arrested, a Department of the Environment investigation was announced, and FINCO shares fell like a stone. The Count then bought them as they fell and, within days, controlled the company.

In a last desperate attempt to save the company, Frank Lutz met with the Count. They met in the lobby of the hotel. Nick ordered them coffee.

"Mr. Chamov, you promised to support FINCO in this deal. If you do not pitch in your support now, you may destroy the company in which you are a major shareholder. We shall all, yourself included, lose everything."

Nick smiled. "Mr. Lutz, I am not the fool you take me for. I have sold all my shares and have shorted many others."

Lutz was aghast and shouted, "You! It is you who has destroyed the deal!? Why? What on earth reason can you have?"

Nick forced himself to keep calm. "Mr. Lutz, do you remember Nicholas Cameron?"

"Yes, I think so. Why? What has he to do with this?"

"Everything. Everything. What happened to him?"

Lutz was baffled. "He was an interfering nuisance. He was sent to Russia and was involved in a deadly car crash. This was many years ago."

Nick almost laughed. "No, he wasn't. There was no deadly car crash. He was taken prisoner and sent into the depths of Russia's ghastly prisons. Where he spent ten years of his life."

Lutz screwed up his face and stared. And gradually realised that he was talking to Nicholas Cameron. "Nick? Not Nicholas Cameron?!"

Nick nodded and told him, "You've lost your company, you may be nearly bankrupt, and you will have to face actions for all your deceitful criminal activities."

Lutz got up and staggered away out of the hotel.

· · • • ·

Later that day, Nick got a phone call from Carmina, wanting to meet urgently. Carmina wanted to meet in a private safe location of his choosing. Nick insisted on meeting in the hotel lobby. As they sat down for a coffee, Nick saw two elegantly dressed thugs sitting across the room, almost watching.

Carmina launched into the issue. "I now know who you are. I know what you have done. I do not want to talk about the past. We need to talk about what is happening right now. Your actions are destroying a wonderful company and bankrupting many of your contacts."

Nick nodded and wondered.

Carmina leaned forward, almost threateningly. "You need to be aware of the forces we have at our disposal. I have many contacts with groups who will carry out severe actions at my request. Also, there are Russian forces prepared to take immediate action. You could save the situation right now, for us and yourself, by using your surprising funds in the right way."

Nick nodded again.

"But you have to act today!"

Nick wondered whether Carmina understood the market. "You're too late."

"NO! It's never too late."

"FINCO has collapsed. It is in the hands of an administrator. Your shares are worthless. An insolvency practitioner is selling your shares. I am working with the administrator to try to save the company. I am investing into FINCO on the understanding that the previous ownership is disbanded and dissolved."

Carmina looked broken.

Nick was quiet but persuasive. "You are now nothing. I remember you telling me to – 'Get a life!'"

Carmina almost shouted, "Then we shall take action against you!"

Nick saw the two thugs stand and start to walk towards them. Several guests looked nervously across at them.

Nick bravely responded. "To no avail. You cannot get anything back. And all your activities have been plotted and recorded. The records will be released if any action is taken against me. The CIA is very interested. You will not just go to prison... So... Get a life."

Carmina held a hand up, and the thugs stopped coming. Carmina slumped back. "But the Russian..."

Nick interrupted. "The Russian, Koshevoi, has not lost all his wealth. He has lost a great deal. He took great care to try to stay somewhat out of the disaster. He did not want to lose his access to British residence and his British assets. However, the KGB seems to have access to much of his recent activities."

CHAPTER 43

WAS IT ALL A DREAM?

That night Nick had one of his recurring nightmare dreams. He relived a terrible night in his lock-up cell. Lice-laden, bed-bugs crawling, no windows, no ventilation, no air, dirty floors. Companions who are broken down crazies surviving only with some fragmented memories. They are his family for a few helpful moments.

Then in a crowded, not much larger cell with fourteen 'friends' squeezed into seven square yards in such a way that they all have to bend their legs at the same time.

But the dirty floor, the murky walls, and the suffocating smell of the latrine bucket do not entirely overwhelm. Because he has fellow prisoners with thoughts, ideas, spoken memories, and shared experiences, that makes a life and allows thoughts of perhaps another life still to come, maybe. They were not his enemies; they were travelling the same road.

Nick, terrified, would wake up again but then try to build some hope. He tried to think about the future and wondered once again about revenge. Revenge?

He repeated his thought. "If you wrong us, shall we not re-venge? Did they wrong me? Who did the wrongs? And if they did, shall I revenge? Does continually studying revenge keep my wounds green? Would I be better to ignore and forget? Revenge is its own executioner."

And where does Joanne come into the story? What role did she play? How involved was she? Does she know anything at all about what went on? Will I find out? Why do I keep remembering... "Don't go, don't go. I'll never see you again."

Did she know something? In the park she had said, "I know."

He then fell into another disturbed sleep. He visualised a confrontation with Jonathan and Joanne. They sit casually in front of him in their luxurious living room and smile confidently. He barely controls his temper and bursts out a slew of accusations. Jonathan gets up and elegantly scoffs and smiles. Nick pulls out a gun and aims it at Jonathan. Joanne screams, "Don't! Don't!"

"You bastard! You were involved in everything all the way along. You knew what was going to happen to me." Nick waves the gun in the air. "You just wanted me out of the way so you could have Joanne. And they wanted me out because I was uncovering their dirty criminal plots and manoeuvres! Aren't I right?"

Jonathan smirks. "Nothing to do with me, mate. All your problems. You're just a loser!" He shouts, "Put up with it!"

Nick shoots Jonathan in the chest. Jonathan collapses, and Joanne screams. Nick grabs Joanne and says, "Get our daughter NOW. We're leaving together, all together!"

She shouts, "YES. Yes. Let's go!"

He wakes, shouting, "Let's go!!"

Then he really wakes and says, "It's all a dream. A dream!"

He gets up to get a coffee. He opens a letter from Anna. She reports that she has had contact with Alexei. And she has arranged for Alexei to be able to leave Russia and come to Italy. She urges Nick to return to Italy, where she says he belongs. And to meet properly with Alexei.

Later, Jonathan calls and asks whether they could talk things over. He invites Nick to their house.

Nick is eager to meet but concerned about how he might behave. But he agrees to come for an evening drink.

He enters their glorious home, almost shaking with anxiety. He admires the paintings in elaborate gold frames adorning the walls. He notes expensive antique and modern furniture competing with each other.

Jonathan and Joanne both greet him formally and stiffly. They look desperately nervous but behave with studied calm. They offer him a drink. He refuses.

"Lovely house you have here. Must be worth a few bob now?"

Jonathan looks like a broken man. "It better be. We have to sell to help us survive the huge catastrophe we are facing. We have lost everything."

Nick nods but doesn't look sympathetic.

"Lutz has told me that you knew exactly what was going on and haven't lost a penny?"

"Correct."

"Had you heard the news about Lutz?"

Nick shook his head.

"Apparently he shot himself. He's dead."

Nick is not surprised.

"Nick, I need to come clean with you. Tell you all I knew, and all I now know."

Nick nodded. He saw Joanne nodding vigorously.

"Lutz and Carmina built up and launched FINCO with funds stolen over time from the bank. I knew nothing about this at the time."

Nick said, "Apart from my suspicions? Which you passed on?"

Jonathan looked down.

"And from where else did funds come?"

Jonathan reluctantly said, "Significant funds came from an outside investor."

"A Russian?"

"Yes, a Russian."

"Is the name Koshevoi?"

Jonathan is astonished. "How did you...?"

"He is the son of General Koshevoi, who had my grandfather, Grishaka, and the first husband of my mother, Nikolai Zharkov, taken out and shot."

Jonathan is astonished and flounders. Eventually, he reveals, "Koshevoi funded FINCO to provide a vehicle for KGB infiltration into influential businesses in the West. But when Gorbachev and perestroika emerged, he changed to using it as a personal exit vehicle for himself and his fortune to the West."

Nick persists, "And you knew all of this and went along with it all?"

"I was just a convenient figurehead. I wasn't fully aware of the frauds and the Russian involvement."

"Koshevoi's involvement has been reported to the KGB. He has been shipped back to Russia to face serious charges. Almost certainly, he will spend a few years in jail."

Jonathan floundered. He pleads, "Joanne, back me up. Explain my innocence and how desperately we need support to save our family and our children. All our children."

Joanne leaned forward and looked him directly in the eyes. Nick looked back, softening.

"Nick, I did not know what had happened to you. I was told that you were killed in a serious car accident in Moscow. I thought I had lost you forever."

Nick believed her.

"I found I was pregnant. Jonathan was very incredibly kind and understanding. Jonathan also thought you were dead, and offered to marry me, because he cared for me, and for the sake of the child.

"Nothing to do with your having been granted large wealth by the American ambassador's father and Jonathan finding that his elegant British gentlemen persona was achieving very little?"

Jonathan muttered and looked away. Joanne got angry.

Nick carried on, "And so Polly... is...."

Jonathan and Joanne nod.

Nick looked at them, his head spinning. He still wanted revenge. And he wanted Joanne. And he wanted his daughter.

But then, Nick realised it was all too late. Joanne was no longer a mixture of rich, spoilt extravagance and rebellious independence. Joanne was a different person; she was now a materialist, no longer a broad-minded potential lefty. And Nick, too, was a different person; the world itself had changed, values were different now, and his daughter had been brought up a different person to the one he would have known.

He turned and walked out of their lives.

He went back to Italy and to Anna, and to meet with Alexei.

SOURCES

YALTA VICTIM   Zoe Polansk-Palmera

VICTIMS OF YALTA   Nikolai Tolstoy

THE GULAG ARCHIPELAGO   Alexander Soltzhenitsyn

ONE DAY IN THE LIFE
OF IVAN DENISOVICH   Alexander Soltzhenitsyn

TALES FROM THE DON   Mikhail Sholokhov

AND QUIET FLOWS THE DON   Mikhail Sholokhov

THE HORSEMEN OF THE STEPPES   Albert Seaton

THE LAST SECRET   Nicholas Bethel

INTO THE WHIRLWIND   Eugenia Ginzburg

COPING WITH RUSSIA   Robert Daglish

A WORLD APART   Gustav Herling

THE HARVEST OF SORROW   Robert Conquest

ABOUT ATMOSPHERE PRESS

Founded in 2015, Atmosphere Press was built on the principles of Honesty, Transparency, Professionalism, Kindness, and Making Your Book Awesome. As an ethical and author-friendly hybrid press, we stay true to that founding mission today.

If you're a reader, enter our giveaway for a free book here:

SCAN TO ENTER
BOOK GIVEAWAY

If you're a writer, submit your manuscript for consideration here:

SCAN TO SUBMIT
MANUSCRIPT

And always feel free to visit Atmosphere Press and our authors online at atmospherepress.com. See you there soon!

ABOUT THE AUTHOR

ROD TAYLOR was born and spent his childhood in Argentina. He completed his secondary and University education in the UK. Since then he has lived in London, Bristol, and briefly, Mexico. He started writing this book in the 1980s. Recently, after further research that is evident from the list of sources, he has completed it. In the meantime he also earned a BA in Literature at the Open University, developed and ran several exciting businesses and wrote another book, a thriller called *A Very Long Shot*.

Printed in Great Britain
by Amazon

29767616R00138